Invisible Thoughts

Chapter 1 Walton

Life can be challenging, especially with A.D.D (My stupid attention disorder). Most people doubt the disabled, make fun of us. It's just not right. What if we doubted the people without disabilities? If the disabled made fun of them? Then the tables would turn. Just like the tables in this story.

Every day as I arise from my sleep, my mind's out of place thanks to A.D.D. I stumble down the stairway of my family's two story house and plump my behind in my usual seat at the family table. During breakfast, my food misses my mouth but I keep munching anyway. My mother comes into the kitchen, prepares some cereal for herself and sits down next to me.

"I hate Monday's." My mom confesses this every Monday morning. So do I, but by actions, not words. My mom starts to talk about her job as an accountant and the drama at the bank

A Nanowrimo Novel

where she works. I listen for about a minute or so, then my mind wanders off, thinking about math class with Mr.Stevenson, the time of the school day I enjoy.

"Hey." My mom snaps her fingers at me. There goes my A.D.D once again. I will last about a minute in dialogue with someone until my A.D.D takes over and my minds off to the next thing.

Today is a gloomy day as I walk out of the Coy's Household. The houses bright accent is shaded by the dim light of the morning sky. When I look up, the clouds seem to separate, wander off.

Just like eight year olds would do, the cracks of the sidewalk are off limits for me. I pretend there is huge crevices with rushing water and sharp rocks ready to break me in half if I fall. My imagery is far more complex than the eight year old's "Break your Mom's back" skit.

Invisible Thoughts

As I'm walking down the sidewalk towards my school, I watch my fellow peers skateboard their way to the school. Next, my attention is pulled by the Toyota Prius making its way down my street I live on. The license plate read **"MRMATH".** Then it hits me. That's my math teacher Mr.Stevenson on his way to school. I wave to him just as he waves to me. It's a morning ritual between the two of us.

By the time I make it to school, I'm one of the last students there, right behind the skateboarders that I saw earlier. The peacocks painting stands firmly above the school entrance as I make my way in the school. Lockers line the walls of the main hallway. Students surround them like bees around their hive, trying to push their way in.

347. My locker number. I unlock the stronghold of my school books and stuff my bag in and take my textbooks and notebooks out. When I close my locker, I try to scurry off.

A Nanowrimo Novel

But we all know what comes next in these type of stories. It's the bully. In my case, Thomas Grueling.

As I'm prancing along, Thomas and I meet eye to eye. This starts the battle with the same outcome. Walton gets shown up by Thomas.

Next thing I know I'm pushed from behind, falling to the floor. The blow of it all makes my nose bleed and the left side of my face goes numb. I turn on to my back to take a look at Thomas. His shaggy black hair sways in front of his left eye. His brown eyes match his brown tee and leather jacket. His jeans sag a little, even though his belt looks as tight to the point you can't slip a paper clip through it. As he laughs, he walks backwards, then turns around to walk to his first period and nudges his friend beside him. When I start to gather my textbooks and notebooks, a new girl scurries over to me, getting on her knees to help me out. Great, I think, don't do it, don't make a scene, Thomas will find out and you will be next.

The new girl looks at me with a concerned and confused face. "Are you ok?" Her voice is soft and quiet, I could barely understand her. She passes me my notebook.

" Yeah, I'll be ok, it happens every morning, like a tradition to Thomas."

"Thomas is the bully here?"

"Yep."

"What's your first period?"

"Language arts with Mrs.Abagail."

"Me too."

"Follow me then."

The new girl follows me to language arts just a few steps behind me, taking the scenery in of Peacocks High School, her new school. What's her name?

Every time I enter Mrs.Abagail's classroom, the bright curtains she has for the classroom blind me for a millisecond. She's the only teacher that has curtains instead of shades for her classroom. She tells us it makes the classroom just that much more picturesque. To us students, it's a excuse for being distracted or not paying attention all though she caught on to that quickly this year.

I take my front seat in the right corner of the room near the door I entered. The new girl sits beside me. My nose has stopped bleeding by now, thankfully it wasn't that bad of a bloody nose.

Mrs.Abagail arises from her desk chair, her pink, floral pattern dress sways left and right as she makes her way around the desk. Mrs.Abagail leans on the front of her desk, arms crossed and starts her every day ritual speech.

"Welcome back again today students, to language arts! I shall be your teacher, Mrs.Abagail!" Her voice sounds graceful and joyful. Joyful to be here.

Mrs.Abagail surveys today's seating arrangement her eyes going left to right. When she looks satisfied, she starts to come towards me. Her eyes wide and along with her wide smile. She stops at the new girl's desk leaning against it like she does everything else.

"Hello sweetie, and what do you go by?"

"Shayla, Shayla Blue."

"Then I welcome you, Shayla Blue, to Peacock High School!"

Shayla. That's her name. I thought it would be something like Christina, Dakota, or Ashley. Shayla's blonde hair is pulled back in a ponytail, she has blue eyes just like mine. Although hers are brighter, brighter than baby blue. She wears a lime green tee and brown khakis. A weird combination.

"Class." Mrs.Abagail starts "Please pull out your homework from last night on Stephen King."

I don't get why she makes us study famous writers instead of teaching us grammar and literature skills. I guess every teacher's different.

Before Mrs.Abagail goes around to collect homework, she grabs a stack of yellow papers off her desk. Detention papers to be precise. It's always the same every time, you don't finish your homework, you shall get detention.

Out of the twenty three of us in the class, six detentions are passed out. I'm not one of them. Shayla is given the homework paper though and lectured on what to do with it.

Today, Mrs.Abagail has chosen for us to learn about Jean Craighead George. She wrote the Newberry Medal Book titled *My Side Of The Mountain.*

With assistance from my A.D.D, my mind wanders off to a world of my liking. A world where everything is perfect. I live in a mansion with pet lions, my favorite animal. I sit in my peaceful and serene garden, reading my favorite book, *A Different World.* By Ethan J. Lane. Then I snap back into reality, to language arts class.

I look over to Shayla. She looks enthralled by Mrs.Abagail's choice of an author. Every second or so Shayla will look down to take notes. I tried that once but was caught for doodling, I can thank my A.D.D.

The next minute I'm looking out the window, there are teens outside at the baseball field with Mr.Sulphuric playing what looks like an intense game of kickball. Thomas is next to kick. Thomas delivered a kick that will surely get him back home. The center fielder runs in for the catch and starts to position himself. Next thing you know, the center fielder is taken out by the ball. I muffle my laugh by stuffing my mouth with my pencil. Next thing I know, class is over.

I make my way out of the language arts room at a slow pace, not wanting to be stuck by the doorway with the strong, mean, pushy students. Shayla acknowledges me and puts her self behind me. In a couple seconds, Shayla and I are out of the classroom, heading to who knows where. We stop outside of the room across from the Language Arts room which is the astronomy classroom. Shayla starts to talk.

"I think we have the same schedule, do you have math next?"

"Yep, and for third period you have U.S History?"

"Yep."

"Follow me once again."

"I'm right behind you."

"And nice to meet you Shayla."

"And nice to meet you...uhh"

"It's Walton, Walton Coy."

"Pleasure to meet you then Walton Coy."

When we enter the math room,
Mr.Stevenson has a tennis ball in his hand.

"Think fast Walton!"

Mr.Stevenson slowly throws the ball at me.
As I catch the ball I'm laughing. Mr.Stevenson
is awesome. I'm always the first to math class,
today I brought Shayla with me. Before the
other students get to the classroom,
Mr.Stevenson and I play pass.

As I throw the tennis ball back to
Mr.Stevenson, he starts to talk.

"What's your name?" He throws the ball
towards Shayla. Shayla catches like she's a
pro at catching a tennis ball in a math
classroom.

"It's Shayla, Shayla Blue." Shayla runs to
the middle of the class room with the ball in
hand then throws it towards me. I catch it one
handed and quickly make it fly to
Mr.Stevenson, who catches it then gently
tosses it on to his desk chair.

"Nice to meet you Shayla, glad you could be part of me and Walton's daily game. Why don't you come early tomorrow too so you can play again?"

"I can't see why not." Shayla seems amazed to have witnessed a game of pass with a math teacher. But around here, anything is possible, or so everyone likes to believe.

Chapter 2 Walton

As I wake up this morning, something feels different, it's like I feel more happy. Then It hits me. This is what it's like to have a friend. Well, I think I have a friend in Shayla Blue but how would I know? I just met my so called "friend" and only know that her name is Shayla Blue and she's a girl. Maybe she just saw me as a mentor for her first day at Peacock High School. Or as a friend? I guess we'll see today.

This morning my mind doesn't feel out of place. Maybe I'm so overwhelmed with the thought of myself having a friend that my A.D.D just doesn't want to ruin it. My food doesn't even miss my mouth! This is new!

When I walk outside today, I find myself in a nice sunny day with clouds here and there to shade the sun. The small, gentle, breeze feels well on my body and it goes well with the heat.

This morning, I don't worry about the cracks of the sidewalk knowing it's a good day and I'm to old for it anyway.

This is the part of the story usually when the plot is all good things, every thing goes uphill. But then I know not to get to excited about this new, great day, because when you go uphill, you come back down sooner or later.

When Mr.Stevenson's Toyota Prius starts to come up behind me, I prepare a big smile to go along with my big wave. To make a show of it to Mr.Stevenson that today is a great day. Instead, Mr.Stevenson makes a show of it.

Mr.Stevenson pulls up next to me, his car slowly moving beside the sidewalk as I walk.

"Hey little boy, I've got candy in my car, it's not utterly strange or anything." Mr.Stevenson starts to chuckle as he speaks his last words of his sentence.

"Stranger Danger!" I joke

"See you second period Walton, and bring that girlfriend of yours."

"Shayla is not my girlfriend! Just a friend!"

"Woah! That was short tempered of you Walton! Why are you so defensive about her!"

"Have a nice morning Mr.Stevenson."

"You too Walton." Mr.Stevenson Pulls back on to the road. *I will have to kill him* I think. *I just will have to kill him.*

This morning when I reach school ground, I'm surprisingly one of the first students there. I enter the school and head for my locker. By the time I grab my books and other school stuff, about only 10 other kids have entered the school. None of them being Thomas but, one of them being Shayla.

As I pass Shayla to get to the Language Arts room, we make faces at each other. I stick my tongue out as she goes cross eyed. We both laugh.

I pass my homework in immediately to Mrs.Abagail and take my normal seat. I start to talk.

"What are we doing today?"

"Starting to develop stories for Nano-Wrimo."

"What's Nano-Wrimo?"

"Nano-Wrimo is a novel writing project."

"We are going to be writing novels?"

"Yep. With fifty thousand words."

"You're kidding me I hope?"

"Nope."

"We haven't learned about Aesop and his fables yet. That should come first right?"

"Nice try Mr.Walton."

"Can't blame me for trying. Now what about Aesop and his fables?"

"Irrelevant question Mr.Walton."

"I'll shut up now."

"Sounds good to me Mr.Walton."

"Again, how many fables did Aesop write?"

"You said you would shut up, remember that Mr.Walton?"

"Irrelevant question Mrs.Abagail."

Mrs.Abagail and I look at each other. We both have very serious faces on. Then we break out into laughter once I raise my eyebrows at her like she does to the kids that don't behave in class.

After the laughter in the classroom dies down, Shayla makes her entrance and sits next to me, just like yesterday.

"Good Morning Walton and Mrs.Abagail."

"Good Morning Shayla."

"Good Morning."

Shayla starts to speak again.

"What are we doing today?"

"Learning about Aesop's Fables."

"No Walton, were starting Nano-Wrimo."

"That was once again irrelevant Mrs.Abagail."

"Will one of you just tell me what were doing today?"

"Aesop's Fables"

"Nano-Wrimo."

"No, Aesop's Fables."

"Nano-Wrimo for the last time Mr.Walton." "Fine Mrs.Abagail, you win today, because I allow you to."

Shayla has finally caught on to our game and asks

"Mrs.Abagail, what is Nano-Wrimo?"

"A novel writing project."

"We are writing novels?"

"Yep. With fifty thousand words."

"Sounds fun."

"It will be."

Language seems to go by fast. We go over what Nano-Wrimo is and how we will have to do a lot of preparation before we start writing. Some preparation is like developing your protagonist and antagonist, creating conflict, and developing plot.

Next is math class with Mr.Stevenson. Me and Shayla hurry down the hall towards the math classroom.

We enter the math classroom, place our school books at our desk, then spread out to play pass. Mr.Stevenson quickly jumps out his chair and next thing I know, the tennis is airborne. I make a dramatic catch and pass it to Shayla. She laughs as the tennis ball reaches her palm.

The three of us play pass for another minute or so. I find it funny how every day a forty year old (or around that age) math teacher gets so eager to play pass with two juniors. Like I've said before, every teacher's different.

Today in math class, we start a new topic. Advance algebra. Mr.Stevenson starts a lecture on how he hopes we payed attention in pre-algebra because that knowledge comes in handy. Lucky for me, when we went over pre-algebra in the eighth grade, I was out with the flu. Life can be challenging. Especially for me. Luckily, Mr.Stevenson didn't give us homework.

The day seems to go by fast, just like my mind, fast paced. From one thing to the next in a matter of minutes. It's the end of the day, one more period, home economics. With none other then Thomas Grueling.

Shayla and I walk into the classroom. This time it's me after her. Shayla and I sit in the front of the class, at the table farthest to the right, near the door. After Shayla and I get situated, in comes Thomas.

Thomas places his behind right behind me. *Are you kidding me?* Before class even starts, Thomas starts in.

"So Walton, how do you like the Language Arts assignment, you have to write a novel, how does that sound?"

I'm ready to take you out at the knees Thomas, shut up.

"What's your novel going to be about Walton Coy, space aliens?"

One more word Thomas I swear.

"It will be hard with your A.D.D, won't it Walton Coy?"

How does he know about my mental illness? I will kill him. At the least, I will make him feel like a idiot for saying that out loud. I raise my hand up high enough in the air to make my self feel bigger then the Empire State Building.

"Yes Mr.Walton?"

"Well Mrs.Willow, Thomas keeps distracting me by talking in my ear about my mental illness."

The class starts to whisper and murmur to the kids sitting next to them. I stand up, and do a slow 180 walking turn to survey the class.

They look at me with faces that tell me I'm a freak.

"So what, I have A.D.D, deal with it."

I sit back down and attempt to move on with life. Shayla seems to try the same thing. She wasn't making fun of me like I thought she would about my A.D.D so I highly respect her of that. Same with Mrs.Willow.

By the end of Home Ec, Thomas has a detention.

Chapter 3 Shayla

I don't know what to think of Walton. Even tough I just met him two days ago, I see him as a friend. As I'm on the school bus, making my way back home, I ponder over what happened with Thomas and Walton today in Home Ec.

I barely know this Thomas kid, but it seems like he can be a real idiot. I wasn't going to join in with Thomas. Making fun of the disabled is definitely mean and something I would never do. My brother has cancer. He gets the "poor you" treatment *every* day. He also gets made fun of by the other fourth graders in his class. Just like Walton being bossed around and being made fun of by Thomas Grueling. No wonder why I have so much sympathy for Walton Coy.

By the time I get off the bus it's around three pm. I'm the last off my bus, last dropped off. Since I started school at Peacock High, my brother started to have his chemo after school which is dismissed at 2:30 pm. At my brother's first consult with his doctor here in Peacock, California, the doctor said that his chemotherapy treatments would only take about an half a hour everyday. They usually get home by 3:20 pm. As I walk into my family's house, the beige walls and tan furry carpets instantly hit me with a wake of boringness. I plump my butt onto the recliner and pull my phone out of my back pocket.

"How did school go today Shayla?" My dads voice makes this boring feeling turn to an even more boring feeling. But I respond every day to his normal parent question.

"Went okay, we are starting to plan novels we have to write in Language, in math, we started advance algebra, (for me it's not hard at all since at my old school in Greenland, Ohio I was in Gifted and Talented for Math, but for others, it looked challenging.) and today, in Home Ec, Thomas was making fun of Walton about his A.D.D."

"Is Walton ok?"

"Yeah, he confronted the class with the telling of his A.D.D disorder. He seemed angered but yet proud of himself for standing up to Thomas."

"Is Walton your boyfriend Shayla?"

"Eww, no, Walton is just a friend I made at school."

"Shayla, you finally made a friend, and on the second day at your new school, it's great you've finally made a friend."

"I guess so."

"What do you mean you guess so?"

"I mean that I just guess so."

"You thirsty Shayla?"

"Pepsi please."

My dad emerges from the blue kitchen with a can of Pepsi in his hands. After my brother was diagnosed with Osteosarcoma two years ago, my mother practically banned sodas. But my dad and I have always found a way around this ban even if it means making desperate measures.

I did not see it the first time, but he has two cans of Pepsi, one in one hand and one in the other. He throws mine to me, this is what he calls my after school physical test. Catching my after school Pepsi before mom gets home. Thanks to Walton and Mr.Stevenson, catching the Pepsi today is no problem. I even manage to catch the cold, slippery beverage with one hand!

Dad sprawls across the couch next to the recliner I sit in. I hear his Pepsi snap open then the television blur on. I crack open my Pepsi and take a sip which turns into a medium sip that turns into a big sip. I have about half of my Pepsi left. I take a look at my dad. He's flipping through the television channels like the Tasmanian devil on a sugar high. He takes a sip of his Pepsi when he lands on our channel we love to watch. The history channel. Awesome right? My dad and I are the new nerds of Peacock, California. On the history channel is a documentary on Adolf Hitler, a past German dictator. He was dictator of Germany durning

WWII. He also lead the Nazis of Germany during the Holocaust. He was a effective leader but with bad actions and ideas. My dad thinks the same. Great minds think alike.

We stuff the empty Pepsi cans to the bottom of the recycling bin by the trash can, not wanting mom to see them. Next I head down to the basement with the open Pepsi box that holds my dad's and my soda stash. I place them in the bottom of the deep freezer. Then, the worst event at the worst time happens. Three of the Pepsi bottles in the box start to freeze and crack open. Soda pours out everywhere. I panic. My mother and brother will be home any minute now. And we have an exploding can massacre going on. I look around in the basement and find some rags by the treadmill that my dad and mother use. I quickly grab the rags and speed back to the freezer. I stuff most of the rags in the box of Pepsi cans then use the rest to wipe the mess up. *Woah, that was close!* I think.

As I make my way back up stairs, my mother and brother pull into the driveway in her silver 2013 Toyota Camry. My dad and I get back to our usual after school routine. Or what my mom and brother think our after school routine is.

My brother walks in, lugging his school bag through the doorway of our house. By the looks, it seems like my brother gets the same boring feeling as I as he walks into the house. He drops his school bag at his feet and whips his sneakers off. My dad looks over to him and smiles from the kitchen. My brother smiles back. Now my brother looks back to me, as he sits down on the couch where dad sprawled out with his Pepsi in one hand, and the remote control in the other just a couple minutes earlier. Now, it's my brother siting up with amazing posture and nothing in either hands.

"Shayla, did you get me that book yet?" My brother looks at me with his hopeful eyes. You can tell his cancer is worsening. He's been wanting this book from the nearby "Book Place" store since school started and he saw another kid with it. He started his school year the first day unlike me. You think with his cancer, he would be the one starting late but I'm not a complainer.

"Well Zachery, I'll make sure to put that on the top of my list for tomorrow. I'll go there right after school." My mom breaks in on my last word.

"Shayla, I'm not letting you walk to a bookstore about half of a mile away from here all by yourself."

"That's ok, I'll get Walton to go with me." I regret it the millisecond after I say it. My parents won't let me go the bookstore with my so called friend I just met. Especially seeing he's a boy. Next is my dad to make a remark.

"Well ok, but if you are on the news missing or killed by this so called friend Walton, you will never leave this house again."

"Dad." My brother wants in on this conversation.

"If she was killed, she will not be leaving the graveyard right?" My dad answers my brother.

"She won't even be leaving her coffin Zachery."
My brother keeps the conversation going between
him and my dad.

"And what will you do with Walton the Killer?"

"Rename him Walton the Dead."

"Who will kill him?"

"A boy named Zachery Blue the Killer."

"Will he be Zachery the great after that?"

"No he shall be Zachery Blue the Amazing."

We all let out little giggles. Even though we all
know that conversation wasn't that funny. But I
guess it's settled, Walton and I are heading to the
bookstore tomorrow.

Tonight we have Cordon Blue Chicken for
dinner, my least favorite dinner I have ever had in
my life. My dad and brother wolf the chicken down
in no time flat. My mom and I take a little longer,
lingering over our chicken.

"Tomorrow night, I'm making dinner." remarks
my Mother.

"Please do." I reply in a low voice.

After dinner, I decide to finish the documentary on Adolf Hitler since my Dad and I paused it before dinner started. With about twenty minutes left of the documentary, I start to drift off, dreaming of what will come the next day.

Chapter 4 Walton

Today, my arrival at school is met with dirty looks and laughs. Even though I am one of the first twenty there, just about all of them make some mean comment to me. By the time I make it inside the Language Arts room, I am greeted by Shayla and Mrs.Abagail. I shoot them both a gleeful smile and a good morning as well.

"You know Walton," Mrs.Abagail starts, "I was reading the first paragraph of the rough draft of your novel and it was pretty astounding. Same with yours Shayla."

Shayla and I look at each other happily that Mrs.Abagail likes the start of our novels.

"I feel you two have the most potential for finishing this novel assignment so I would like you guys to stay after school to work on them with me so they can be astonishing! Are you fellows staying?" Now Shayla starts to speak.

"Well, I may be a little late because I have to go to the bookstore to get my little bother a book he wants very badly. Now to say that, Walton, my parents said I could only go if I take a friend with me and my brother really wants this book so are you willing to come?"

Shayla looks at me with a hopeful face. I am surprised that she sees me as a friend. I reply to Mrs.Abagail and Shayla.

"What about we schedule our first novel writing meeting tomorrow Mrs.Abagail?"

"Sounds good to me Mr.Walton."

I reply to Shayla's question.

"I will text my mother at the end of class Shayla."

"Sounds good to me Walton." Shayla replies.

The rest of the day comes and goes at the high school. The pass playing in Mr.Stevenson's room went as usual and surprisingly during Home Ec, Thomas went home sick. It was a pretty uneventful day with

the exception of language, math, and home ec.
Now its time to go to the book store with
Shayla.

There are five minutes left of study hall.
Every thing is peaceful and serene in
Mr.Woodstock's (My homeroom) classroom.
That is until Mr.Stevenson comes in.

"Walton, to the hall please, we need to talk
and you are being dismissed." Mr.Stevenson's
voice is very jumpy and excited. Why?

I gather my school belongings and head to
the hall with Mr.Stevenson. Am I in trouble?

"I am giving you and Shayla a ride to the
bookstore." remarks Mr.Stevenson. I decide to
reply.

"Students can not leave with a staff member
off school grounds during school hours
Mr.Stevenson."

"We will be fine."

"No we won't."

"Do you not trust me?"

"I trust you just that-" Mr.Stevenson starts to cut me off.

"You trust me, then let's go."

I no longer fight back to Mr.Stevenson. He won. He is driving Shayla and I to the book store.

To my surprise, Shayla didn't even fight with Mr.Stevenson. She agreed right off. The three of us leave right away.

Shayla took the passenger seat so I was squished into the back of the small puny Toyota Prius. This car is a joke.

The inside of the Prius is small and I am claustrophobic. This is just great. The seats are black leather with brown leather rims. The buttons and other gizmos light up like neon signs in the front of the car. Mr.Stevenson puts the car in drive and were off.

We play the radio on the car drive to the bookstore even though we are only a couple minutes away. Mr.Stevenson has it on a channel that plays classical music. I don't like classical music and by the look on Shayla's face, she clearly doesn't either. But we play along seeming it was nice enough of Mr.Stevenson to take us to the bookstore.

Mr.Stevenson parks his small car in the front of the store just like my dad does. The three of us pile out quickly like we have not had fresh air in eons. To me, it was nearly realistic.

When we enter the store we are hit with all the books surrounding us. The kid section is to our left, bright with yellow and pink bookshelves and toddlers running about or sitting in beanbags and other funky seats. We head to the right. The teen section.

The teen section is less colorful. It's black and gray shelves creating a boring and tired feel. I ask Shayla what book she is looking for.

"*A Different World* By Ethan J. Lane" replies Shayla.

My mind shifted into the world of Ethan J. Lane's novel. My favorite novel. It's about a boy named Ara Keghart and he has a special power called electro kinesiology. A power in which controls electricity. In the community he lives in, everything is near perfect. There is a cure for cancer, no mental illnesses, no physical illnesses, no crooks, everyone is allowed their opinions. Mr.Lane should have titled his book "A Perfect World" but that I guess didn't come to his mind.

Without even telling Shayla or Mr.Stevenson I storm off to the shelf I know holds Mr.Lane's book. Shayla makes an effort to grab my arm but she quickly just let's me wander off. After about thirty seconds, I'm going to the checkout by myself with Shayla's brother's book. I buy it myself.

After a minute I find Shayla and Mr.Stevenson still standing in the same place, probably still waiting for me. I hide the book behind my book until I get to Shayla. I stop a couple inches away from her, smile at her then question her.

"Guess what I have?"

"A surprise?"

"What type of surprise?"

"The gift type I'm hoping?"

"Ding! Ding! Ding! We have a winner! You reward is this book!"

I pull the book from behind me, shoving it towards Shayla's hands. She gladly takes the book.

"Walton, you payed for the book?"
I look at Shayla with a gleeful smile and say, "I sure have."
Shayla just looks at me for a couple seconds. Then Mr.Stevenson cuts in.

"Hey you two, I need to get you guys home, let's go."

Shayla and I follow Mr.Stevenson out the door. I am stuffed in the back of the car again. We pull out of the parking lot, back on to the main road. I start to speak to Shayla.

"What's you're brother's name?"

"It is Zachery."

"I want to meet this Zachery sometime soon."

"My parents will be fine if you come over for dinner you know."

"You sure?"

"Yeah, just tell you're parents you will be at my house for dinner."

"Okay, I will text them right now."

"Walton?"

"Yeah?"

"Just a heads up, my brother, well he,"

"Well he what?"

"He has cancer."

Mr.Stevenson pulls the car over, out of traffic. This rush of sadness and guilt goes through me all at once. I can only manage to say a couple words. The same words that Mr.Stevenson says right after me.

"I'm so sorry Shayla."

"Me too Shayla, I'm so sorry."

Shayla responds right after Mr.Stevenson says sorry.

"Thank you, and Walton listen to me."

"What?"

Shayla looks back at me with a straight face.

"Zachery does *not* like the "poor you, you have cancer." treatment, you got that?"

I can she how much Zachery means to Shayla. I get her point that she does not want me to give Zachery the "poor you" treatment, so I nod to let her know I have comprehended what she said. The rest of the car ride to Shayla's house is quiet, very quiet.

Chapter 5 Shayla

Tonight for dinner is mayhem with a side of Walton. Sounds crazy huh? It is. For actual food, tonight we are having sirloin steak with steamed broccoli and dinner rolls. My mom cooked so it is actually decent food.

Walton and Zachery are on a roll. When Walton and I got here, Zachery started to read his new book and got a couple chapters in before dinner seeming how fast of a reader he is. Now, he and Walton have been talking here and there about the book during dinner. They talk about this boy with eletro kiniesology and how he plans to take away electricity from the greedy by absorbing it with his powers so they can learn better. Meanwhile in this boys part of town, everything is perfect. Literally.

"So Walton, are you Shayla's age?" my dad has been looking at Walton and giving him the third degree when he's not debating with Zachery. Walton has caught on to my fathers trick and keeps killing him with kindness.

"Yes sir I am, we are also in all the same classes."

"Is Shayla good in class?"

"Yes sir."

"And you?"

"Yes sir I sure am."

"You a bully?"

"No sir."

"Thats very good Walton, do you have good grades?"

"Yes sir, I sure do."

"Where do you live?"

"Next street over, Pine st."

"Any siblings?"

"No sir."

"Do you have both parents?"

"Yes sir."

"And, nice to meet you Walton."

"And you as well Mr.Gregory."

The conversation between my dad and Walton finally ends by the time everyone has finished their meals. Zachery scurries off to read his book while Walton and I sit down to watch television. Walton slouches in the recliner and I sprawl across the couch. My dad and mom sit in the love seat. We all watch the NFL game with the Philadelphia Eagles against the Chicago Bears. The Eagles are winning 13-12 in the last couple minutes of the third quarter. I don't really understand football and neither does dad or Zachery but Mom and Walton get all into it.Walton is rooting for the Bears saying that the referees are favoring the Eagles while my mother is chanting "Eagles are going to win! Chicago Bears are going to cry!"

At the end of the third quarter, I walk into the kitchen and plop some popcorn into the microwave. Walton and mom have been demanding more popcorn almost each 10 minutes of the game. This is around their fifth bowl of popcorn. I prance back into the living room with the bowl of popcorn and leap away as I place it on the coffee table, knowing mom and Walton's hands will reach at the bowl right away.

We haven't heard from Zachery since dinner since he went to his room to read for a while. I decide to go give Zachery a visit.

Zachery's room walls look like a stretched out map of the world. He loves geography and maps. I haven't been in his room at the new house yet but now I can see why he likes to hole up in here so much. He closes his book when he sees me enter.

"I like my maps, it seems like everything revolves around me when I am in here you know?" Zachery looks at me with an enthusiastic look.

"It is a pretty unique room for sure Zachery."

I turn around wondering where the voice came from. Walton is standing in the door frame, leaning against it. Walton's light brown hair is scraggy but yet neat. His blue eyes compliment his blue polo shirt and khakis. His grin reaches both sides of his face. Zachery starts to reply to Walton.

"Sure is."

Walton prances into Zachery's room and pulls out the desk chair from beneath the desk. He takes a seat almost as quick as the chair came out.

Zachery reaches over to his nightstand and grabs a stress ball with the design like it is Earth. I get the idea that he wants to play pass.

"I'm open!" yells a serious Walton.

Zachery laughs and passes the ball to Walton. Just then I remember telling Walton and Mr.Stevenson about my brother's cancer and made sure that Walton wouldn't talk about it tonight. Walton is keeping the job I gave him and doing it well.

"Shayla." Walton quickly whips the ball at me.

I make a dramatic catch by diving onto Zachery's bed the moment my hand makes contact with the ball. Zachery knows it is coming and I easily pass the ball to him. He bobbles the ball but manages to catch it.

We sit in Zachery's room playing pass almost all night. Sometimes Walton would crack jokes about this novel writing project we have to do and how he is a not a good writer and why would Mrs.Abagail want him to stay after school to work on it.

Every other minute or so, Zachery would spark a conversation with Walton about the book he is reading. They mostly talk about why would the main character have special powers but no one else? Walton clearly knows the answer because he read the book before but plays along for Zachery's sake.

The room becomes quiet after a while. Walton has stopped cracking jokes about Mrs.Abagail and Zachery has stopped trying to spark conversation. Are they waiting for me to say something? I do not know.

Then I look over to Zachery. He does not look like he is in good condition all of the sudden. Did playing pass tire him out? Is it just that his cancer makes him sleepy?

All of the sudden, Zachery lets out a obstreperous scream. Zachery curls up into a ball on top of his bed. He screams again.

"My leg! My leg!"

Walton and I take action. Walton quickly takes out his phone to call 911. Walton leaves to room for a more calm place downstairs. My parents scurry in.

"Walton is calling 911 right now." I say

"What happened?" Questions my worried mother.

"He has serious pain in his leg" I reply

My dad just looks at Zachery then to me. He is the only one not taking action.

Zachery just lies there in a ball and cries, cries, cries, and cries. I hope it is nothing to serious.

"The ambulance is on there way." hollers Walton from downstairs. Mom, dad and I just stand their for a second. Then it hits me.

"Mom, Zachery has Osteosarcoma in his left Tibia and Fibula right?"

Mom just looks at me for a second then replies.

"Yes, he may have to get his leg amputated."

Chapter 6 Walton

Shayla is not at school today which does not surprise me. Last night before the ambulance got there, Shayla carried Zachery down and laid him on the couch. Shayla and I exchanged phone numbers so she could keep me updated on Zachery. She texted me this morning and said she stayed the night with Zachery at the hospital and that they amputated his leg right away last night. He may be getting a prosthetic leg but they have not decided yet.

Today as Mr.Stevenson and I play pass, it seems lonely. I am thankful that Mr.Stevenson doesn't ask me if I know why Shayla isn't here today. He just looks at it like a regular absent student which is an everyday thing at any school.

In math class today, we have a pre-test on advanced algebra. I know their is no way I will even get a sixty on this test but I try my best.

Today is just a tornado of confusion for me. Shayla sends me a text before Home Ec. that reads "Zachery woke up a while ago, my parents and Zachery decided on a prosthetic leg. Meet after school at my house?" I text back saying I will come over after I'm done with Mrs.Abagail today with novel writing.

Thomas isn't even in Home Ec. today. That's weird, he made fun of my face in the period before then in the hallway. His partner in crime that usually sits with him is also missing. I shake it off my mind.

"Class we need to have a talk." starts Mrs.Willow

"It was just announced a couple minutes ago that last period, Thomas Grueling and Lucien Leopold wandered out of the school and went a couple streets down and got high on drugs. They both died of an overdose sadly, but, this is a lesson that you should never do drugs. Today we will have free time or you can work on your homework if you have any. I'm sorry for those in this class that were close to Thomas and or Lucien."

My mouth just hangs open. I can not believe what I just heard. I pull my phone out of my pocket and text Shayla "Thomas and his buddy died today of a drug overdose, Home Ec. is quiet. Very quiet. We have free time though. So it will get loud in a minute." Shayla replies almost instantly texting "You are kidding me.

That is not good. Even though he was a bully it is just crazy."

Shayla and I text for the most of Home Ec about Thomas and his friend Lucien. Also every other text is about Zachery. He got fitted today for his leg by Shayla's information.

All of the sudden, something runs into me. I turn around to see this smaller junior boy with glasses. He looks to me like a nerd or geek.

"I am so sorry." The boy pleads as if he is scared of me. For some reason, he looks like he is.

"It's okay." I say "The names Walton, yours?"

"Callum. Nice to meet you Walton." Callum lends me his hand to shake it. I take it without ease.

"Nice to meet you too Callum."

For the last couple minutes of Home Ec., I talk with Callum and come to really like his way of handling things. He was also bullied by Thomas a lot and actually stood up to him on multiple occasions. I tell Callum about Shayla, Zachery, and also being bullied by Thomas. He seemed to listen well. At the end of class, we exchange cell phone numbers to keep in check with each other.

I walk into Mrs.Abagail's room with as much happiness as I can muster. Most of it coming out of Callum and my conversation.

"Quite the day Walton, I'm sorry about everything. Shayla called and told me about Zachery and their is Thomas and I knew he was a bully towards you."

Shayla has shared phone numbers with a teacher? That I have never heard of.

"So forget about all that for an hour Walton and let's start your novel. Title?"

I need to think about that for a minute. I decide I want my novel to be on kind of what is going on now with Shayla, Zachery, Thomas, Lucien and Callum.

"Lost." I reply "My title is Lost."

"Ok Walton, what is the inciting incident?"

I think on that one for a while too. I ponder different ideas in my mind but finally settle on one in particular.

"The main character is taken hostage by the antagonist. The main character never finds out where they took him until the falling action."

"Very good idea Walton, the climax?"

This one does not take me as long as the other two. It sparks right away.

"The boy is able to make an escape after a week of planning. On the way out, he saves a younger girl."

"It sounds interesting Walton. The Only thing you really changed from the lay out sheet you made is the title, is their a problem with the other title?"

"Nope."

"I like your new one a lot more."

"Thanks."

"Walton for your first after school novel assignment, I want you to write a very confusing, questioning, detailed first paragraph ok?"

I nod to show I know what I'm suppose to do. I tear out a piece of lined notebook paper from my notebook. I start to write.

I try to make every word mean something, even the articles. I found out that was not possible. I start with a quote. A quote from "A Different World" By Ethan J. Lane. I made sure to tell where the quote is from.

After about 5 minutes, I have finished my first paragraph to the best of my ability. I arise from my seat and walk over to Mrs.Abagail's desk where she waits patiently for me. When I pass the paper over, all she can do is smile at me before reading it.

Mrs.Abagail's eyes quickly scan the paper. She smirks at me as she raises her head from the paper.

"I believe you have potential with this novel Walton, I really truly do."

She passes back the paper and I am a little reluctant to grab at first for who knows what reason. As I grab the paper, I think about how this novel can keep my mind off everything that is going on in till it is all cleared up. The perfect distraction.

As I think of distractions, I think about my A.D.D. It seems to be getting better. Maybe with all this commotion I do not even notice it if it kicks in. I suddenly have an idea in my mind. I decide to ask Mrs.Abagail.

"Mrs.Abagail?" I ask

"Yes Walton?"

"I was wondering if I could come tomorrow and bring someone with me?"

"I can't see why not Walton."

"Really?"

"Yeah, I do not mind one bit."

"Same time, same place Mrs.Abagail?"

"Yes Walton, that sounds good. You are dismissed."

I leave the room rather quickly wanting to ask Shayla so many questions about Zachery and how he is doing. As I walk over to her house I decide to ask only a couple questions that are not to personal so I do not overwhelm her.

Also on my walk over, I think about Callum. Could he be a friend? I guess I do not know just yet. This makes me think of how quickly Shayla and I became friends. Could it be the same case with Callum? I laugh at myself out loud knowing this is stupid.

When I reach Shayla's door, I give it a couple knocks. Nobody answers. I give it a couple more knock and then Shayla comes to the door.

Shayla opens the door and smiles.

"Come on in." She answers

I immediately make myself at home like I have been here everyday of my life after school. I have only been here once.

"How was school?" Shayla asks likes she is my mother.

"Good, how is Zachery?"

"Good. So about Thomas and Lucien?"

I just pause for a minute. I look down to the ground and think about all the things Thomas has done to me. I also think about why someone would name their kid Lucien. Weird thought but whatever.

Shayla seems to be doing the same thing as me when I look up. Except she probably is not thinking about the name Lucien and how weird it is. Shayla starts conversation again.

"How was novel writing with Mrs.Abagail?"

"It was great, she had me write my first paragraph so she could tell me how to start a story."

"Great. I will be there tomorrow. I promise."

"Ok."

"So, want to play a board game?"

"Sure, why not. Which one?"

"Monopoly?"

"If you insist on losing Shayla."

"Walton, I will pound you to sardine size pieces, even a little smaller."

"Game on."

After I finish saying "Game on," my phone goes off in my back pocket. It's Callum. He texted "Want to hang out right now?"

I decide to reply right away. "Sure come to Cumberland Lane."

When Shayla and I start playing Monopoly, she quickly takes the first three properties around her. For me, I wait four turns before buying a property, I end buying the Boardwalk after four turns! I got lucky!

I haven't told Shayla who Callum is and that he is coming to her house because I invited him. I decide to keep it secret until someone "randomly" walks on to Shayla's lawn.

"Walton? Who is that?" A nervous Shayla questions

"Oh, that's Callum, an acquaintance I made today at school in Home Ec."

"Why is he here?"

"He wanted to hang out, is that ok?"

Shayla just looks at me with a curious look that is saying *What's Next?* I kill her with kindness and shoot a smile her way. Next thing you know, Callum is banging at the door. Shayla shoots a smile and decides to answer the door.

"Is this Callum?"

"Yes, is Walton here?"

"Yes he is, come on in, we were just playing some Monopoly."

Callum starts to make his entrance inside Shayla's house when he asks, "And who are you?"

Shayla smiles right at Callum then responds, "I am Shayla, Walton invited you to my house to hang out unexpectedly. Walton is my friend."

The house goes silent for nearly a minute. Everybody is frozen like their encased in a block of ice. To break the silence, Callum laughs like a clown and then Shayla and I join in.

Shayla and I put away Monopoly and turn on the television. Callum takes the couch, sprawling across the seating. I take the recliner, putting the foot rest up for max comfort. As for Shayla, she takes the love seat sprawling across it like Callum on the couch.

To all of our's surprise, we watch Luny Toon's re-runs for a whole 4 hours until Shayla's dad get's home from the hospital and announces Shayla's mother will be staying with him tonight.

Shayla's dad grabs us all a can of Pepsi saying he and Shayla will share their stock just this once but, Zachery and Shayla's mother can never know there is Pepsi in the household of the Blue family.

Shayla's dad didn't really pay much attention to the new body in the room. He seemed happy at the fact that we were happy.

At around Nine P.M, Callum and I left. We ate dinner there as well not wanting to go home to no friends. Callum says he has a younger sister in Elementary school. She is in the 5th grade. That is as close to a friend any of us have at home. I guess Shayla has Zachery but right now he is in the hospital. I should really give him a visit. That is what I am doing after my consult with Mrs.Abagail.

I will go see Zachery and maybe, his new leg.

Chapter 7 Walton

I wake up this morning very tired. My alarm clock beeps away. I try to ignore but just cannot. I pound my hand around my nightstand, trying to hit the alarm clock. It doesn't work.

After the pounding was finished, I decided to just get up. I try to shut the thing off, but it won't shut up. I have no better solution but to throw it out the window, so I do.

I quickly open up the window. I take the screen out and pull it in. Next step, the alarm clock is out the window. Just what I wanted.

I peek my head out of the window to watch the fatal blow. It scatters into pieces, making a clanging noise. I grin at my work.

I get dressed and make my way downstairs. Today, I am wearing a green plaid shirt and boot cut jeans. I also have a Chicago Bears NFL cap on, to show that even though they lost the other night, I will still show team pride.

I drag myself downstairs, just barley walking. I plump myself in my usual seat. Then, I remember that I am downstairs for breakfast so I get back up and prepare myself some cereal. I sit back down again.

As I eat my cereal, I think about Callum, Shayla, and Zachery. I invited Callum last night to come with Shayla and I to Mrs.Abagail's class after school tomorrow but he said he had to go to Thomas's funeral. If Callum was bullied and hated by Thomas, why would he go to his funeral?

The next of the three to come to mind is Zachery. I need to pay him a visit today after my novel writing with Mrs.Abagail. I feel bad for the kid. I actually feel like I bonded with him so much when I was at his house for dinner. I wonder how he is doing with his book?

Shayla is the last of the three to come to mind. I think she is also wary about Callum and how he is going to Thomas's funeral. Shayla's best guess is that he was Thomas's drug dealer or something of that sort. I do not believe her, I think they are distant cousins.

The last thing to pop into my mind this morning is my novel. Ever since yesterday with Mrs.Abagail after school, I have been very excited to write my novel. This makes me think of the dedication page. Who should I dedicate my novel to?

As I am leaving the house on my way to school, rain is pouring down. And, to top it all off, I was last to leave the house so when I locked the doors, I locked myself out until I get home after school when my parents unlock the place. For the past 2 years I have tried convincing them to get me a key to the house, but they refuse.

I have no better idea but to run. I start with a slow jog, then a more steady running pace, next thing I know, I am sprinting along the sidewalk.

I start to hear a car coming up behind me. Little do I know, it is Mr.Stevenson pulling up along side me. I wave as he stops next to me. I decide to stop too. I am not that wet but will be if I stand here any longer. Nearly every time it rains, I do not get that wet. It is weird.

"Walton get in the car! Your'e getting a ride!" Hollers Mr.Stevenson from his car window. His long, curly, beard, looks soaked from the rain even though he is covered by his car.

As I am getting in the back seat closest to the sidewalk, is when I see Shayla in the front seat next to Mr.Stevenson. She wears a purple rain coat from The North Face Company and bootcut jeans. Her jacket is unzipped, revealing the blue long sleeve shirt beneath.

"Dummy." Remarks Shayla. I know she is talking to me when she turns her head to see me cramped up in the back.

"What?" I reply

"Where is your rain jacket?" questions a laughing Shayla.

"Well, I, um, forgot it." I slowly reply

"Really Walton, Really?"

The rest of the ride to school is about politics and how we have to vote for a new governor of California. Right now we have the Democrat Karen Russell. She is trying to get re-elected for her second term in office while the other two candidates are both retired senators for the state of California. Brian Morgan, the Independent candidate is probably her biggest rival. David Daniels, the Republican candidate, is not expected to even get ten percent of the votes.

"I believe Governor Karen Russell has the best ideas for our state and is the only worthy candidate of being in office this time round." Shayla speaks her opinion very fluently towards Mr.Stevenson. Mr.Stevenson starts to chuckle at Shayla's opinion.

"What?" Asks Shayla

"Well I believe that Brian Morgan is the right choice because he is honest while Governor Karen Russell lies and says so many negative things about Brian Morgan and David Daniels. She is a total idiot." Mr.Stevenson smiles, happy to get his say out. Shayla turns to me and asks me to be the tiebreaker.

"David should go into office." I say. Shayla and Mr.Stevenson look blankly at me. They then turn to look at each other and start laughing. Mr.Stevenson is laughing so hard he pounds his fist on the steering wheel. When Shayla is laughing she just looks at me. She then starts to speak but, I cut her off before she can end her first word.

"You two will see, the underdog will win."

"Yeah, right." Says a sarcastic Mr.Stevenson. For the rest of the ride to school I stay quiet, not wanting to interfere with the two politicians conversation.

Of course we are early to school because, what teacher isn't? Shayla decides to camp out in Mr.Stevenson's room until school starts and I decide to pay Mrs.Abagail a visit.

Today, Mrs.Abagail is wearing a striped, black and white shirt. She also wears black dress pants for lower clothing. She supplies a gold and silver necklace around her neck and pearl earrings.

"Hello Walton, why are you here so early?" queried Mrs.Abagail

"Got a ride from Mr.Stevenson, decided I would hang out here till first period if it is okay with you." I say everything so quickly I do not even remember saying it.

"Woah! Speedy Gonzalez! Sure you can, but slow down when you talk!"

"Okay."

"You have to promise one thing." Starts Mrs.Abagail

"What?"

"That you work on your novel."

"Okay I guess."

I pull out my school laptop and start to work on my novel. I have copied my first paragraph on to the computer. I have also finished a couple pages since then. I have been working at night on it, getting a good five hundred words in every time I type. It's weird how all kinds of ideas just flow into my mind with every word I write. I feel I am pulled into the world of my novel and can not leave. I feel I am Aaron, my main character and that I am the one that later on, will be kidnapped. Sometimes, I see myself as the kidnapper, Ricardo, plotting the future kidnap of Aaron. Very little, I feel as a ghost, dead, useless character, just watching it all lay out. Right now in my social life I feel that way. I feel with the mystery of Callum and Thomas, Zachery's cancer, I am the outsider in this case. In my life story right now, I see 3 conflicts. One, is that Thomas and Lucien passed away and Callum's weird connection to them.

Another is more of Shayla's conflict, but I feel is mine. Zachery. He is the second conflict to me. I honestly feel awful for the kid. Like it was my fault for engaging in pass and probably made him tired. *Doofus.* How did that make his leg hurt?

Anyway, my third conflict is my novel. Most importantly, the dedication page. I know it is to early to think about that part of my novel but I do anyway. Part of me wants to dedicate to Zachery but then the other part wants me to dedicate Mrs.Abagail for the help of putting it all together. This hasn't happened in a while, but my A.D.D made me drift off to the point I haven't typed one single letter since I thought about all of these things. I shake the thoughts off and direct my thinking on my novel. I can't. I am now thinking about my A.D.D. I think about how much better I have been able to control it and forget it is there. With me twenty four seven.

When I actually do type a letter, first bell rings and it is time to start class. *Stupid.* All my peers pile in one by one. Shayla comes in and sits in her usual seat next to me.

Mrs.Abagail gives me a quick look, to tell me that I should have been writing rather than daydreaming on and on and on and on. For a response, I shrug. I do not know what else to say.

I glance over to Shayla. She shoots me a smile. I smile back. Her blonde hair is pulled back in a ponytail, making her blue eyes stand out. Her clothing appearance has not changed since the car ride except her not having her rain jacket on.

Today, we work on plot development for our novels. Mrs.Abagail has been telling all the kids that this novel stuff is just for practice, that not everyone has to write a novel. In fact, I am the only one writing a novel. It will be fun. I guess.

Chapter 8 Shayla

After school, I head straight to the hospital to see Zachery. He is getting out tomorrow. Yesterday, he got his prosthetic leg on. He has been messing around with it ever since he got it on.

I walk into Zachery's hospital room when he is reading his book. He is almost finished. Amazing. He just got the book a couple days ago and he is already to the end. When he catches sight of me, he puts his book down and jumps right out of the bed.

"Zachery, be careful." remarks my mother from the corner of the room. I never saw her until she spoke.

Zachery just shakes his head to ignore her. I give him a quick side hug.

"I am going to get something to eat, will you be okay here Shayla?" My mom looks at me with a face saying *please let me go eat.*

"Yeah," I reply "Go eat, we will be fine."

My mom throws her purse over her shoulder and heads out the door. Zachery and I both wave to her. When she is out of sight I turn to Zachery.

"Shayla, you and Walton need to go to Lucien Leopold's funeral this weekend." Zachery quickly spits out.

Why? How does he know about this?

I decide to play along because he does read the newspaper and searches the web.

"Why is that Zachery?"

"Because they say Lucien and Thomas's drug dealer is a relative of Lucien's and will probably speak at the funeral. You need to go and put him in the slammer."

I immediately think of Callum. He said he was going to Thomas's funeral. Is he going to Lucien's? I need to get Walton on board with this right away. As much of a coincidence as it is, Walton walks right into the Hospital room at the moment I finish my thought.

"Walton, I thought you were staying after school with Mrs.Abagail tonight?" I ask

Walton lets out a long sigh and then decides to answer.

"Took the night off, wanted to come see Zachery instead."

I feel it is very of nice of Walton to come see Zachery. Walton is still in his clothing from school. He also wears a smile on his face as he sits on the edge of the hospital bed.

I think Zachery's funeral crash idea is brilliant if Walton and I can pull it off. Walton and I just need to dress nice, like most people do at a funeral.

We sit in silence for almost a minute. Next thing to break the awkwardness, Zachery tells Walton about the plan. Walton nods as Zachery goes along. Smiling at some parts of the plan. Honestly, I only heard about the funeral crash part when I arrived at the hospital. I did not realize Zachery had planned the whole thing out.

Walton and I leave together at around four P.M when my mother gets back. She also ended up doing a little shopping. For the last half an hour Walton and I were there, Zachery and Walton talked about the book. I bet more than anything, Zachery has the book done by the end of the night. As I walk outside to the hospital parking lot, the wind gently makes my hair sway back and fourth. I look over to Walton as he flips his cellphone out of his pocket.

"Calling my mother to pick us up, we can hang out at my house for a while." Says Walton.

I nod over to him in response. We are both juniors and still do not have our licenses. I almost got my license back in Ohio, I was doing really good driving up until the parallel parking at the end.

I was so close. I wonder if Walton ever tried getting a license.

After about fifteen minutes, Walton's mother pulls up to the sidewalk by the hospital. Walton and I have been sitting on the bench outside waiting patiently for our ride. The bench is old and the paint is worn. It is a wooden bench, the structure and back are metal though. It has (or had) a navy blue color paint job on it. A weird color to paint a bench, if it is normal to have a painted bench.

Walton let's me have the front seat and he takes the back. His mother's car is a black Honda CRV, there is leather seats on the inside with a black color as well. The dashboard is lit up with technology and buttons, like most cars nowadays.

"Hello Shayla," Starts Walton's mother. "Nice to meet you."

I smile at Walton's mother. "Nice to meet you too Mrs.Coy."

The ride ends up to be very loud. We sing songs all the way to Walton's house. I do not know where this urge to sing came from, but it surely came.

Walton's mother acts like she has known me all her life, she is already very comfortable around me. Which makes me comfortable around her.

I look out the window for a brief second to catch my breath from singing. The trees quickly fade away as we come by them but new trees take there place. As we stop at a red light, I turn my head but, something catches my eye and I turn my head back towards the window. Walton and his Mother still sing away but I keep my attention focused on the person I am looking at outside. I know that I have seen him before. He takes looks to his left and right before going down a deep, dark, ally way. He puts his hood up and starts to make his way down the ally way. I see something sticking out of his pocket, it looks like a drug of some sort. Walton's mother starts to drive off as the light turns green. That is the last I see of the boy going down the ally way.

The boy reminded me of Thomas and Lucien even though I do not know either of them well seeming they passed.

I know we are almost to Walton's house because the small city like place of Peacock, California fades away slowly.

I know who that boy is, it is Callum.

Chapter 9 Callum

I take a sharp turn left than a sharp turn right. The way to my bosses hideout is far more than complex and I am one of the few to know the way.

I make my way to a screen door. I nearly take it off the hinges when I rip it open.

Inside the old apartment building is an empty lobby. Well at least to most people it would look empty but for me, I know all the secrets. I go behind the receptionists desk and get on my hands and knees. Nobody knows there is a panel on the flooring unless you are my boss or work for him.

I knock three times on the panel. Then twice. Then once.

"Come down!" yells a voice from below the panel.

I reach in my pocket and pull out a key. I insert the key into the lock holding the panel to the floor. When I hear the click of the lock, I take the key and place it back into my pocket. I throw the panel up and it reveals a hole beneath.

As expected, their is my boss waiting for me at the bottom of the ladders that lead into the basement type room.

My boss has a buzz cut. His hair is brown, the same as his scruffy, five o' clock shadow. He wears black cargo jeans and a white tank top. Their is also a black, leather jacket covering the tank top. He has a cigar in his mouth, it's not even lit.

I make my way down the ladder and close the latch above me, locking it from the inside. When I am fully down the ladder, my boss starts to speak.

"Well Callum, looks like we lost two of our most important customers because of you."

What?

Next thing I know, boss has me pinned to the floor, a knife sitting on my throat. I gulp.

"Boss sir," I start. "It is not my fault they don't know how to manage their drugs doses. Cut me some slack. Holy shit man."

I know boss will cut me some slack. I have a weapon against him. I know his real name. For years, he has gone by Junkie Jack. He moved here from miles away in Chicago, Illinois. He made the big bucks in Chicago selling drugs to those of the thug life 'round there. But in Chicago, their was competition for him. After a while he didn't make as much money so he moved to San Francisco, California, re-starting his business.

While he was in his second business, he nearly was caught. He had only two goons to help him in San Francisco, or so he says. The goons were caught by the cops while Boss made it out, not ever seen. His next stop was here.

He now has seven goons, I am one of them. I am his so called second favorite goon. His favorite overall is Eric Watson. He was the first of the seven goons in the small, city like part of Peacock, California.

Boss's father was also a drug dealer. Way far out in Alaska. I find it funny he moved their just to sell illegal shit. He left my boss, his wife, and my boss's two other siblings, both girls.

Anyway, after my thoughts, I decide to risk calling him by name. Which will probably take him by surprise. At least I hope or else, he may actually kill me.

"Don't you dare Benson Stanford pull that knife any closer to me or I will snap it in half."

Benson looks totally taken back by me calling him by his real name and not Boss or Junkie Jack. And the part about me breaking the knife in half is probably true, it is only a small, Bear Gerber, pocket knife, a sixteen dollar cheapie.

To my surprise, he brings the knife closer to my neck. Unlike last time, I don't gulp knowing the knife is so close it could make a cut if I do.

Benson is on top of me, my arms are pinned by his knees, my legs free, that give me an idea to get out of here.

I kick my left leg up really quickly into his butt making him squeal in pain. His knife clatters to the stone or cement, or whatever type of floor it is.

As I am scrambling to my feet, I grab the knife an hold it securely in my right hand. I point the knife at Benson.

"Not so smart now, huh Benson?" I try my best to mock his voice but don't do that good of a job as I was hoping.

He is trying to crawl backwards away from me scrambling towards the wall behind him. Once he hits the wall, I have already had time to figure out what to do next.

I come closer to him, still putting the knife between him and I.

"Give me your key to the place." I order

"Never." Coughs up Benson. He sounds scared for once.

I point the knife towards his face and walk towards him. He then gives up both his keys. One to the hideout entrance, and the other to the cabinet in the back corner of the room that holds the drugs.

"This world has always been a dictatorship," I lecture. "And now is the time I take over with force, scram you piece of shit."

He scrambles to get on to his feet and slowly walks to the ladder. He turns his head just enough so I can see the side of his face. He starts to climb up the ladder.

"Well played Callum, but, this isn't over, I have forces you don't know about, unspeakable power. We will definitely meet again. I can promise you."

I push him to the floor to climb up the ladder and unlock the hatch for him. I climb back down.

"Get." I harshly protest.

Benson lets out a grunt and climbs the ladder. I never see him again. Never.

Chapter 10 Shayla

Zachery is coming home today. I sat through all my classes today, excited to have him back home.

Nobody knows that I saw Callum go down that dark ally way. I am planning to go there, bring a clueless Walton and see what is going on down there. It's only about a twenty minute walk from Walton's house to that street I saw Callum on anyway.

Right now, I am in study hall. There is fifteen minutes left of class. I am pretending to read my book but, really, I am thinking about the two plans. The first one is Zachery's plan for crashing Lucien Leopold's funeral and discover his weird connection with Callum. The second one is my plan to go down that dark ally way to see why Callum went there.

I look over to my side to see Walton. He is working in math homework. He is scribbling like crazy on the paper, trying to get it completed. You can tell he does not like to have homework.

He catches me looking at him and shoots me a smile. I shoot one back. He is wearing a red polo shirt and jeans.

Walton and I thought about getting our families together for Thanksgiving seeing most of both of our families do not live near Peacock, California.

My family mostly lives in Ohio, where I used to live. That was until my mom's boss wanted to move her to Peacock, California, a small serene town near the new bank where she will be working. My mother was a little reluctant at first because of Zachery's cancer and all the family. But then budget cuts came to the school where my dad worked; he was one of the cuts.

My dad was an 8th grade science teacher, a good one. He has a masters in teaching science. It was my dad loosing his job, that sparked my mother to move here. That was about 6 months ago.

The bell rings. I have been thinking so much that I forgot about making it look like I was reading. I dash to my locker and pack my school bag so quick that you could not say "Hi" before I was finished.

I am the first one on the bus. (With the exception of the bus driver, elementary, and middle school kids.)

The middle school kids are saying murmurs of a name I have heard before. Lucien. Lucien's little sister, rides my bus, everybody talks to her about Lucien. I never thought about listening in on the conversations. It could give me more insight towards the Callum case.

I sit right behind Lucien's sister. I try not to make my eave dropping obvious.

"Hey Sarah, is it true your brother had a fake hand?' asks one boy.

Sarah. That is Lucien's sister's name.

"Sure did John." Says a confident Sarah

"How did he lose it?" Questions a boy sitting with this John kid.

"Picture this," Sarah says. "We were on vacation in Florida and we went to a zoo. A crocodile got loose and Lucien fought it. The croc bit his hand off but somehow, Lucien managed to win."

The two boys ooh and ahh at the story. *That can not be the true story.*

The rest of the eave dropping ride home, Sarah does not say much. I still listen desperately, hoping Sarah talks to her self or something like that. Nothing.

By the time I get home, I have not gathered any more information on Lucien Leopold. The fact that he supposedly has a fake hand hit me hard. But with the story Sarah told, I guess I am not that sure.

When it is my turn to depart off the bus, I do it tiredly. I clench my bag in one hand and my book in another. My book bag drags along the driveway of my house, making a weird sound I can not explain. But, if I had to explain it, a kind of sounds like a cat tying to hold onto the curtains with it's owner pulling it off. I guess I could explain it.

I grab for the house key in my back pocket. I open the door and it takes me about five minutes because for some reason, I am so very tired.

The minute I am inside, I drop my schoolbag and book and pull my phone from my pocket as I take my place on the couch.

I bring my knees up to my shoulders as I text Walton.

I ask him this, "Meet me tonight at the gas station that is a couple streets down, where dark clothing and bring your brain."

He responds immediately saying "Okay, can't promise my brain though."

I giggle to myself and reply, "Please do bring that brain, be there at quarter of midnight."

All he texts back is a smiley face.

I decide to take a nap when I finish texting Walton but we never stop. We talk about crashing the funeral and how Zachery is coming home tonight. And little did I know, Walton was on his way here to see Zachery and I.

Walton doesn't even knock, he just barges in like he owns the place.

"Hello Shayla."

"Hello Walton, Zachery should be home any moment." I reply

Walton shoots me a smile and sits on the couch, next to me. The second he sits down, mom and dad pull into the driveway together. I wonder what car has Zachery?

Walton and I both shoot each other looks then race outside. Zachery comes out of my mothers car. I run over and pick him up.

I spin Zachery around and around in the air, he laughs and giggles as I do so.

I set him down so someone else (Walton) can have at him. Walton give him a high five and a fist bump.

Everyone is smiling. Mother, father, Walton, Zachery and I. After a minute or so of the homecoming outside, we decide to move it inside.

Zachery takes the couch and lays down. I take the recliner as Walton takes the love seat. Walton has the remote and turns on the television.

The show to pop up on the television screen is Family Feud. It is the Crayton family v.s the Buds family. It is nearly a tie game, the Crayton family winning. Mother and father have wandered off to the kitchen to make dinner.

Usually, when someone gets home from the hospital, their parents make them have nothing but luxury. I remember when I was sick with the influenza back in Ohio when I as seven years old, they gave me nice warm and cozy blankets for my bed and waited on me. In this case, my brother has cancer and they don't wait on him?

All of the sudden, Zachery gets up and starts to talk in a low voice.

"What should we do? I feel we need to get to the bottom of the Callum case."

Walton and I shoot each other worried looks, does Zachery know my plan for tonight on finding out Callum's secret once and for all?

"Listen Zachery," I say "We don't need to worry about this case ok? Not right now. Just sit back down and watch some television. Please?"

Zachery is a little reluctant at first to sit down but after a second or two, he obeys. I wonder if I should bring him along tonight? I guess Walton and I could add one more to be a menacing trio. Right?

Chapter 11 Walton

I decided to quit the novel gig. I just was not into it. Mrs.Abagail was a little angered but got over it saying it's ok and maybe next year. I finally have a friend and I want to experience every minute of it.

My novel was not that good of and idea anyway. I mean a kidnapped kid, really? I wonder if anyone would have read it?

It is around ten P.M. I left Shayla's around eight P.M. I have a feeling that we are going to see something to do with Callum. I wonder if Zachery knows what is going on?

I have my black attire laid out on my bed. My plan is to walk to the gas station.

My phone is charging. It sits on the carpet of my room so the charger could be plugged in to the outlet.

My bedroom is on the second floor of the house. It has ugly burgundy walls, making the room look like bloody vomit. I nearly vomit every time I enter.

I have a desk on the wall opposite the doorway to enter. A couple of books sit on top of the desk. The desk is made of walnut wood. There is also the newspaper sitting on my desk. Yeah, I read things like that.

I am planning to leave the house by eleven thirty. That will give me fifteen minutes to walk to the gas station.

I just dilly dally in my room, I don't know what else to do. To my fortunate luck, my parents went out to dinner tonight far off in San Francisco, for my mothers work. They are going to stay the night in a hotel halfway home tonight, then drive the west of the way tomorrow. That will leave me free to get out of here quickly.

I look at the calendar above my desk, there are three days till Thanksgiving. Today was my last day of school. I am on break now, this means Shayla and I need to find a way to get our family together for Thanksgiving, and quick.

Another date that is marked on the calendar this month is my birthday, November twenty ninth. I don't know what I will do for my birthday this year but I am hoping to do something with Shayla and Zachery.

I have started to believe Shayla with her theory on Callum and how he is a drug dealer. I bet that is what I was called for tonight, to stop him.

Ten fifteen P.M. I look at my watch in disgust. I wish it would be midnight already and me and Shayla would be on our way to do who knows what.

I decide to head downstairs and get a snack. My phone is fully charged so I unplug the charger from the phone and wall and grab the phone. I text Shayla. this, "Just you and me tonight for this mysterious task?"

She responds a minute later when I have poured myself a cup of root beer.

She says maybe Zachery will be coming along. Great. What we need is a nine year old to hold us back. More specifically a nine year old with one leg.

I grab a snack size bag of salt and vinegar chips and go to the living room. The living room is a yellow and gold kind of color. There are two brown, leather, recliners and a smaller couch that is also decorated with brown leather.

I take the small couch and sit cross legged on top of it. I gulp down the soda and set the cup on the floor to pick up later. I start to woof down the chips one by one. I turn on the television and switch the channel to the late night news that started at ten. They talk about snow coming to the northern parts of California already. *Great.* I live in Peacock, California, one of the most northern towns in California. We are only about an hour away from the state of Washington.

I absolutely hate snow. I love the holidays but hate the white crap they bring with them. I kind of actually fear snow as weird as it sounds. When I was a little kid, me and my father built sort of an igloo out in the backyard. Dad went inside to go get some food coloring to decorate the igloo like base when it all collapsed on top of me.

Ten thirty. When will the waiting game end? The news is half way done. They now talk about this years new governor, Brian Morgan. Mr.Stevenson was right, Morgan won.

Ten forty five. It feels like hours. I switch the television channel to The Game Show Network. Wheel Of Fortune is on.

Eleven P.M. Getting closer. I decide to go change into my black attire. Once I am dressed, I stuff my phone into my back pocket. Then I have the urge to text someone so I pull it back out. I text Shayla a smiley face or two then put the phone back in my back pocket. I feel my phone vibrate a time or two but ignore it.

I take the black, football paint and make stripes under my eyes. I then place the black cap on my head.

Eleven thirty, time to go.

I toss the thought in my head of bringing my bike along with me but decide not to because I may have to ditch it somewhere.

I start to speed down the road, ready to go. I wonder if Shayla will bring Zachery?

I have never gone faster in my life, I will surely be at the gas station a couple mins early. I slow down for a min or two to check my texts. Shayla texted, "Meet behind the gas station by the dumpster."

I respond, "Okay."

I am behind the station in the next minute or so. I made good time.

Eleven forty seven is the time Shayla gets there. I thought my eyes failed me when I saw Zachery limping right behind her. We all sit down out back for nearly ten minutes until Shayla says for us to follow her.

We walk to where ever Shayla is bringing us. The walk is pretty quiet seeming the only one knowing where to go is Shayla.

We come into the more city like part of Peacock, California. Peacock is a pretty big town. Most of it is suburbs and the rest is city like. We are not a famous town. Our school really sucks at sports. The uprising is we have the best academics in the school district.

Shayla comes to a stop at an ally way.

"Follow." Orders Shayla

"I am not going down a dark ally way at night in the city." Responds a reluctant Zachery.

"Ditto." I agree.

Shayla looks at Zachery and I with disgust. She pulls out her phone to look at the time then puts it back into her back pocket.

"Well, hate to break it to you two wimps but, you're going." Shayla looks at us sternly. Her eyebrows are raised about as high as they can go.

I shoot a look to Zachery and Zachery shoots a look to me. Zachery, to my surprise, just shrugs everything off. If the nine year old can just shake this fear off, why can't I?

Shayla starts to jog down the ally way first. Zachery goes next, then me.

Shayla comes to a stop where the path splits into two different paths. She turns to Zachery and me. I know whats coming next. Why did she want us to come with her?

"Zachery is coming with me if we split up." I quickly spit out.

Shayla nods and starts to go to the path that goes forward. The only other path is the path to the right, so that is where Zachery and I head.

Zachery and I keep a slow pace until we reach the end of the path. Now the path takes a sharp left. So we follow it.

"I have a feeling this all has to do with Callum." Zachery limps along at our now, jogging pace.

"Me too." I remark, "Do we need to slow down?"

"No, I am fine."

We go along until we reach a true dead end. The only thing that stands in front of us is a screen door that is barely on it's hinges.

Zachery starts to step toward the door but I put my arm up to keep him back when I hear a couple voices.

"What did you do with boss you little shit?" Says one voice.

"I am your boss, what are you talking about?" Answers back a more, familiar voice.

I hear people coming towards the door and Zachery and I start to panic. I look around us for a hiding place knowing we can't run fast enough out of here.

A dumpster catches my eye and I motion for Zachery to hop in. Zachery is a little reluctant at first, but hops in. I hop in after him and close the top.

We made it in the dumpster just in time when I hear the door slam open. I am glad to only hear one set of footsteps. The person pounds their fists on the dumpster top and makes a dent in it. Zachery jumps at the motion but controls himself.

I think we gave ourselves away though with Zachery's movement.

The dumpster top opens up with a slam and two figures stand over Zachery and I. I guess my hearing sucks because their are two people, not one. The one closest to the left is a tall figure. He has a super small go-tee and wears a beanie cap.

The second figure is all to familiar. It's the skinny, little, Callum. All I can manage to do is keep my mouth shut.

Chapter 12 Callum

I grab the smaller kid as Eric grabs Walton.
The smaller kid kicks and throws a fit. Walton
to my surprise, just is a little reluctant but still
obeys Eric.

Eric and I giver each other a look as we
stand outside the hideout.

Eric motions to the hideout. So I go first and
pull along the smaller kid. But then something
odd happens Eric lets out a coughing grunt as
someone pulls him from behind. Walton then,
kicks him in the gut, breaking free.

As I wasn't paying attention, the smaller kid
got a hold of my arm and now starts to bite me
really hard. I let out a yelp, this kid has power.

I figure out that it was Shayla who helped
out Walton because she comes charging at
me. The smaller kid rolls away as Shayla
tackles me into the receptionists desk. My
vision goes a little blurry around the edges.

I am out of breath so I don't get up. I watch
Walton slug Eric when Eric tries to get back up
on his feet. Eric again goes back down again.

Walton makes his way out the door, gone.
The three of them are gone.

I scramble up to my feet, and bolt through
the door. I hear the three making their escape

so I follow their sound. I make the usual turns in the dark ally way. By the time I make it out of the dark ally way, the three are gone and Eric is behind me.

Eric pulls me back into the ally way and throws me down. My vision is still blurry so I don't try to fight back.

"You let them get away you son of a bitch!" Hollers Eric.

Eric slugs me two more times after speaking.

I start to kick my legs frantically, trying to shake him off. It does not work. Just then, I think of an idea. It is risky but won't hurt me much because I am basically in the worse condition I can be in.

Eric's head comes down to my head, just what I wanted. He starts to whisper something in my ear. I can not make out what he is saying and nor do I care.

I bang my head against Eric's head. He screeches in pain. I next kick him somewhere around the pelvis I think. I am not sure seeming I can barely see.

I start to crawl backwards, away from Eric. I get up in a matter of fifteen seconds. I stumble away from Eric, making my way back home. I think I dropped my key somewhere in the ally way chasing for Walton, Shayla and that smaller kid who bit me.

I forget about the key. Yes, this means I can never get inside the hideout again but, I have new ideas anyway. My new ideas are to get Benson and Eric in jail, and get rid that of trio, especially the smaller one who bit me. That would be nice.

Chapter 13 Walton

Last night, I got back home around two A.M. Lucky for me, my parents gave me a key this weekend for while they were gone.

It is six A.M now and the weekend.

The first thing I thought of when I woke up is Shayla and Zachery. I feel bad for easily letting Zachery get captured. I also know I need to thank Shayla for practically saving my life last night.

I also don't know who that other guy with Callum was. We also never found out what we were there for. Is Callum truly a drug dealer?

I need to keep Callum and that other figure on my mind today because, today, is Lucien Leopold's funeral and Callum is sure to make an appearance.

I am dressed in a black and white plaid shirt and jeans. My shirt is buttoned all the way to the top. I am picking up (Going to her house then walking the rest of the way with her.) Shayla at her house then we will both make our way.

The funeral is outside, making it easier for Shayla and I to get in.

I fear that the guy who was with Callum last night may show up and pound on Shayla and I.

I need to keep my ears perked and my brain working.

By the time I make it to Shayla's house, we have twenty two minutes until Lucien's funeral starts.

Shayla walk outside in a black tee-shirt and dark jeans. You can tell she doesn't like to dress up just as much as I don't like to.

"You ready to go Walton?"

"Ready as I'll ever be."

The walk to the graveyard is pretty quiet. Shayla hums a song and twiddle my thumbs. You can also hear the cars passing by us.

We make it to the graveyard a couple minutes late. That was our plan. Nobody will pay attention to us when they are focused on the funeral. Shayla and I split up. I go to the back of the seats while Shayla goes to the front.

I see Sarah sitting out front with who must be Lucien's parent's as the priest speaks. The parents look all teary eyed as Sarah looks casual.

As the priest finishes his speech, someone else gets up to talk. Callum, to be descriptive.

Shayla looks back to me her face full of worry thinking that other guy is probably here with Callum. I shrug for a response, because I do not know if that man is here.

"Lucien, was my third cousin." Starts Callum. "We were close, very close. Close from the end, close form the beginning. We practically grew up with each other. I am disappointed to hear that Lucien and his buddy, Thomas Grueling were interested in doing drugs and did so. But we all love him the same. Everybody in life makes bad choices, we all have." Callum stops for a minute and starts to tear up. So does almost everybody else. Shayla looks back at me again. She looks back towards Callum when he starts to speak again.

"Now, with Lucien Leopold gone, we have to be brave. As hard as it is, we have to move on. That is what Lucien would want us to do. Am I right"

Everybody nods. I never realized how good of a speaker Callum is. Callum starts to speak for a third time.

"So as I said, we have to move on from Lucien's death, it is what he would want us to do. Thank you for listening to me. For Lucien Leopold."

Everybody starts to get up and move towards Lucien's body to see him. I know

Shayla wants to get in there to hear in on any information that may pop out.

I also move towards the casket to find some information. Not on Callum and Lucien's bond, but on Lucien's fake hand.

Shayla told me the story of the bus ride with Sarah and the two boys. And even as gullible as I am, I did not even believe that story.

All of the sudden I hear a loud thud sound near the casket and a small pop. I run towards the casket and push my way threw to see what happened. Shayla fell on the temporary stairs on the way up to the casket and with the rumble, Lucien's fake hand popped off. I hear someone behind me say, "That is the girl from last night."

I freeze. I know it's not Callum's voice, Callum is by Lucien's mother. It's the figure I have been so weary about.

He must not notice who I am because I am back to him. I move out of his way and help Shayla up on the way.

I still don't turn my face towards him knowing this is already a disaster.

Shayla gets up and says sorry. After a moment or two of everybody staring at Shayla and Lucien's fake hand, the funeral goes on.

Nobody says anything about Shayla and I
just showing up. That helped us out of this
situation, for now.

Shayla and I weave for the crowd on the
way out, trying not to catch any attention. We
make it to the sidewalk in a matter of seconds,
away from the graveyard.

But, we are not the only people leaving this
early. The taller man and Callum come with us.
Catching up. I quickly grab Shayla's hand and
we start to run.

Shayla pulls out her phone and call for her
mother to pick us up at the high school. That
means we will meet Shayla's mother half way
back to Shayla's house and Callum and his
friend will be out of luck.

Callum and the tall man start to catch up to
us. So, we run faster.

I look back occasionally to see how far
away the dummies are. They are close enough
for me to hear them now. But, not close
enough to grab hold of us.

Callum is ahead of his friend by a little and
yells back at him, "You are the slowest person I
have ever met."

The taller man just laughs at Callum when he starts to gain speed and is ahead of Callum right away.

Shayla and I let go of each others hands and sprint as fast as we can as we make it to the school parking lot.

Shayla's mother makes it right when we start to slow down. Shayla and I both quickly hop in the back.

Zachery is sitting in the passenger seat up front and looks back at us and shakes his head in disgust.

Chapter 14 Shayla

Walton owes me big time. I have now saved his life twice in two days. The first time I kicked that mans butt. The second time was just two hours ago.

Walton and I have been sitting on the couch watching The Wheel Of Fortune. Well, I sit in the recliner with the foot rest up and Walton sits on the couch.

Walton turns to look at me. "We need to talk to our parents about Thanksgiving. It is a couple days away after all."

I nod and head to the kitchen to talk to my parents about it.

"Hey mom, do you think us and the Coy family could get together for Thanksgiving?"

Mom and dad look at each other then at me.

"I guess so why not." Replies dad.

"Thanks so much guys!" I say.

I walk back to the living room and sit on the couch next to Walton. He is on the phone with his mother talking abut Thanksgiving.

I quickly grab Walton's phone out of his hands.

"Hey!" Hisses Walton. I ignore him and start to talk to his mother on the phone.

"Hello Mrs.Coy, this is Shayla, we will be hosting the dinner and your family is invited."

Mrs.Coy laughs over the phone.

"I will bring desert then." Replies Mrs.Coy

"Bye Mrs.Coy."

"Good bye Shayla."

I hang up the phone and pass it back to Walton.

"Shayla, I got to go, my parents are almost home from their trip and I want to make dinner for them. See you later?"

"See you later Walton."

Walton dashes out the door so he can go make his parents dinner. I wonder how good his cooking is? Knowing Walton, he is probably ordering take out. I giggle at the thought.

"Shayla." Starts my mom, "Could you please come here for a minute?"

What could this be about?

As I enter the kitchen, both of my parents are sitting at the island bar, filling two of the four seats.

"Whats the problem?" I ask frantically knowing somethings up.

Mom starts to tear up as dad looks straight at me.

"Shayla, Zachery's cancer is getting worse, he isn't expected to live much longer. Maybe till February." My dad looks down, a hopeless look on his face.

I start to cry. Hard. My mother starts to cry as well.

My dad just keeps his head down. The room goes quiet for a minute or two after mom and I finish crying. Then I break the silence.

"Does Zachery know about this?" I am practically shaking all over. I notice when I bring my hand up to wipe away the tears.

"No, he does not need to." Replies my mother.

I head upstairs to my room and close the door. Careful not to slam it just in case Zachery then would come in to see what's wrong.

All I do is cry. Cry for maybe three hours straight. I can not think of a life without my little brother. He is my better side. Even with the big age difference, we have always stuck together.

We are both smart. That is one thing that has always brought us together. They have no G.T programs in Peacock, California, so neither Zachery nor I get to have real advance classes.

I think about last Thanksgiving back in Ohio with the rest of my family. My aunts, uncles, grandmas, and grandpas from both sides of the family.

My Uncle Flynn is the funniest of the whole family. Along with Zachery. The two would always be in sync. Always side by side. The whole family started to think that Zachery likes Uncle Flynn more then my father. I am pretty sure thats true.

The only thing on my mind when I am crying is topics to do with Zachery. How smart he is, how funny he is, anything I can pull deep out of my mind.

Once I start saying to myself Zachery is this, Zachery is that, I know that soon I will probably have to say Zachery *was* this, Zachery *was* that. I slap myself for thinking so negatively.

I force myself to stop crying and clean up my face to make it look like I wasn't crying. It takes me a minute or so to gather my thoughts.

I decide I want to do something with Zachery. Just me and him so he never forgets it.

I want to now do anything Zachery wants to do. Even if it means reading that stupid book that Walton showed him.

Invisible Thoughts

With my luck, I should ask him for his book now.

A Nanowrimo Novel

Chapter 15 Zachery

Shayla told me last night that she and Walton want to take me to the Thanksgiving fair in the next town over. I feel this has a backstory to it all.

They think I don't know but I know. My cancer is getting bad and the word is right out there. What word you may ask? Death.

I lay on my bed with my prosthetic leg in my hands. I don't take my new leg off much but sometimes I do.

I fiddle with the latches of the leg that connect it to whats left of my real leg. I like my new leg. Of course I prefer a real instead of a fake one but I'll take what I can get at this point.

I wear jeans and a polo shirt that is blue. I also wear my loafers. I attach my other leg and put the loafer on that foot two after the crew sock that goes on first.

Shayla walks into my room and motions for me that it is time to head out.

I hop off my bed and follow Shayla downstairs to the living room where Walton is waiting.

"Ready to go Sir Zachery?" Jokes Walton.

"Ready as I'll ever be." I say back.

"Will you two stop the chit chat? Mom is waiting in the car for us." Shayla speaks up.

We could easily walk to the fair. A fifteen minute walk at the least. But, I understand seeming dumb and dumber found themselves in a chase yesterday.

I hop in the back seat of the Camry with Walton as Shayla takes the passenger seat. I can easily tell Walton is claustrophobic by the way he sits. He tries to spread out as much as he can. I laugh at him.

Walton looks at me with the stupidest look on his face and says, "You got a problem with me Mr.Zachery?"

I just laugh at him once again. Walton pretends to be mad at me by giving me this absurd look. I give the same look back.

The rest of the ride to the fair is a Walton and Zachery show. Shayla and my mom laugh at every mean comment we make at each other.

I keep calling Walton a Juvenile Delinquent as he calls me Zach-A-Frass. His name makes no sense. Mine is an actual heard of name though. If that counts as anything in this circus.

We get to use handicap parking at the fair thanks to me. I could get us to that part of having a fake leg.

My cancer started a couple years back. I went to the doctors because I just was in the worst condition. They gave me a pet-scan. My leg lit up like inner-city New York at night time.

That was when torture started. I got chemotherapy every morning before I departed for school.

My cancer was just kind of neutral after a couple months. I basically forgot about it. I still went in to chemotherapy every morning because my old doctor thought it to be terribly bad even though I wasn't in any pain.

Then we moved here. My cancer was still neutral when I got here until school started. That's when I did truly realize how my old doctor said how terrible it is.

"Their is a team obstacle course here, you three should sign up." Mentions my mother as we pay our way into fair.

"We will dominate the competition for sure." Puts up Shayla.

Walton nudges me with his elbow and says, "If we lose, this is all on you Zachery."

I grin.

The four of us sprint to the obstacle course seeming it is starting soon and we need to sign up. Mom is a little behind us, in no mood to run. Same with me because of my leg. I wish I was as fast as I use to be.

Once we sign in, we are assigned a team color (Purple) and sent to the start line. Lo and behold, the team next to us, the yellow team, consists of Callum, a little girl who I think is Lucien's little sister Sarah, and that tall figure that had a hold on Walton the night we went venturing.

Shayla leans down to whisper in my ear as she sees me observe the competition and whispers to me, "And those three idiots, we are making sure they are going down."

This stupid fair may decide the end of the Callum case all in all. Let's hope.

Chapter 16 Zachery

Walton, Shayla, and I decided I will lead the race. To win, the rule is that one part of the body of at least one player from your team crosses the finish line.

For the yellow team, Sarah is leading the race. She looks maybe two years younger than me, not even that.

I have scoped what I can see of the course. The start is just a sprinting section then goes into wall climbing. That leaves two more parts. After climbing down the wall, you get down to army crawl under a net. You get up and sprint to the end of the course.

RING!!! The bell goes off to indicate that we can start. I sprint right off, not worrying about saving any energy. Sarah is only a split second behind me.

Shayla and Walton are right on my heels, obviously keeping up with me. For the yellow team, the taller guy is in front of Callum, who is in last for the yellow team.

I practically jump on to the wall, giving me a good start. I am already two pegs up on the wall after jump my which is a good thing with the down fall of my leg and climbing. This is when Sarah takes over the race.

Once I get to the top of the wall, Sarah is climbing down. I know I will have to jump down to catch up with her. The wall is not that high so I know I can do it. I just don't want to break my prosthetic leg. I close my eyes and jump.

A sting goes though my body and my prosthetic leg rattles and shakes. I immediately get down into a crawling position because the net is right in front of me.

I am ahead of Sarah in the crawling part of the race until I notice my prosthetic leg gets full of mud and slides off my foot. I support it under my arm and keep going. Once I get out of the net, Sarah is already half way through the last sprint section. I need to act quick.

I sit cross legged on the sprinting section and don't move so Shayla or Walton can't stop me because they are under the net still. They just watch me in curiosity. I thought they would be yelling at me.

I throw my prosthetic leg towards the finish line. I don't know if that will count as a body part crossing the line but I sure hope so.

It whizzes past Sarah which makes her run even harder. Everybody is quiet. I thought they would be yelling and screaming at me, telling me I'm crazy. But, everybody is quiet.

I am very weak with the cancer and all, I was never strong anyway. I threw that leg to the best of my ability though. If it breaks, mom is going to kill me because she will have to pay for repairs.

My leg lands and skids across the sprinting section. In fact, it skids across the finish line before Sarah.

Everybody is quiet as I get up on my one leg to let Shayla and Walton out from under the net.

Walton picks me up and he and Shayla walk towards my prosthetic leg.

The man waiting at the finish line to declare the winner just looks at my muddy, broken leg then starts to speak.

"Team Purple, did not actually break the rules, just used them in complex ways so, I declare Team Purple the winners!"

Everybody cheers for us chanting, "Fake leg for the win! Fake leg for the win!" It actually doesn't bother me much.

This proves the world wrong, the disabled have their triumphs too. The most amazing of all.

Chapter 17 Shayla

Zachery kicked butt in the obstacle course last night. All Walton and I did was trail behind him. The only team to keep up with us was the yellow team. And they almost beat us.

I am mostly surprised at the fact that they counted Zachery's prosthetic leg as a part of his body. Maybe they did it out of pure kindness seeing he doesn't have a leg.

Tomorrow is Thanksgiving, and the Coy's are coming as guests. Of course, we are having a turkey for the main course. We bought the turkey at the grocery store as my family is not apt to hunt. The Coy's are also bringing mashed potato, and a surprise desert.

The turkey is thawing in the kitchen while I sit in my bedroom texting none other than Uncle Flynn.

Mom told me when we got home last night that Zachery needs to see all the family and friends he can see before he passes. She left me in charge of getting hold of everyone. So the first person I think of is Uncle Flynn, Zachery's sidekick.

I have tried getting a hold of him all day long but it is just not working. I have his phone number from when I lived in Ohio and we used to talk a lot. Now, with being in California, I have only talked to him once, when we first got here.

I drop my phone on my pillow and lay down on my bed hopelessly. That is when my phone goes off. I quickly perk up and snatch my phone off my pillow. I check my phone, but, it is a text from Walton. I sigh. Walton texted, "Got a HUGE surprise for Zachery tomorrow night, talk to you tomorrow."

What could Walton possibly have in mind?

I am the only one at the house at the moment. My dad is at work at the mill. He would rather be teaching science again but he will take what he can get. Zachery and mom are going to the hospital to get Zachery's prosthetic leg fixed.

That leaves me, alone, with the turkey to keep me company. That thought makes me giggle.

Seeming I can't get a hold of Uncle Flynn, I try my favorite family member, Aunt Mattie.

Zachery has only met Aunt Mattie once in his life while I have seen her on multiple occasions. She is my dad's only sibling and she is a whack job.

My dad does not like her. At all. He says that she is always drunk twenty four seven. She really makes dad mad, thats why she is my favorite.

Mom did say to invite two family members that could make it from Ohio to here before Zachery passes, so I chose Zachery's favorite, and the rich, drunk, whack job.

I don't care if I get in huge trouble from inviting Aunt Mattie, it will be all worth it in the end. It will give Zachery some humor he hasn't had in a long while.

Uncle Flynn is from my mothers side. One of her two siblings. The other is in the Navy. The Navy seal's name is Robin Carcaster. Carcaster is my mother's maiden name. She married my father Gregory Blue, and became a Blue. My mother's name is Cathleen.

My phone all of the sudden rings away. My ears perk as I answer.

"Shayla, is that you?"

"Uncle Flynn!"

"Nice to be talking to you Shayla, how are you doing?"

"Great, what about you?" It feels great to be talking to a family member other then the three I live with.

"Doing ok, what do you need?"

I gulp and start to tear up, it will be hard to tell Uncle Flynn that his sidekick is dying.

"Well, Uncle Flynn, Zachery's cancer is getting worse, not so long ago, he lost a leg to his cancer and he is soon to pass away. It would be really nice for you to come see him."

I hear Uncle Flynn start to cry over the phone. From what I remember, the guy was never really emotional.

"Thanks for informing me Shayla, I will get on the first flight tomorrow morning."

"Sorry Uncle Flynn, and I love you."

"Sorry too Shayla, nice talking to you, I will keep my phone nearby if you need me, love yah princess."

I smile as I hang up the phone. He hasn't called me princess since I was around Zachery's age. My phone starts to ring immediately after I finish my smile. I check to see who is calling me this time, it is, to my luck, Aunt Mattie. I answer.

"Hey girlie! What you up too?"

"Not much Aunt Mattie, I have a question of you though."

"What is it honey bee?"

"Well, Zachery's cancer is getting really bad and I thought you would like to come see him before he passes away which could be any day now."

The phone line goes silent.

"Well honey bee, thanks for telling me this but, I'll have to pass."

"What! Why Aunt Mattie?" I start to get angered at Aunt Mattie. She wont come see her nephew while she has the chance?

"Well sweetie pie, I have met that whipper snapper once and don't really care for him." Now I am really mad at Aunt Mattie and all I can manage to do is hang up.

I remind myself that we still got Uncle Flynn coming for Zachery and thats what matters. I can now see dad's understanding on why he doesn't like Aunt Mattie.

Chapter 18 Walton

Shayla and I have both planned surprises for Zachery tomorrow. Shayla called me a couple minutes ago and said that she is getting Zachery's favorite Uncle to California for Thanksgiving. I still didn't tell her what I am doing for Zachery. It will surely blow his mind.

I check my email over and over again just in case Ethan J. Lane has to cancel Thanksgiving with us. Yeah thats right, I got the author of that book Zachery and I read to celebrate Thanksgiving with us. He has no family any way to celebrate with so I thought this could tie in.

I e-mailed him Zachery's story and how his cancer is getting so bad to the point his time is shortened. To my surprise, he e-mailed me back and said he would be pleased to celebrate Thanksgiving with us and that he will be there an hour before Thanksgiving starts.

All Shayla knows about this is that I invited someone. That's all I told her so she could set out yet another set of utensils and another plate. This means there will be nine of us celebrating Thanksgiving. Three different families in all.

I sit downstairs on the living room couch having absolute nothing to do. I seriously sit there twiddling my thumbs.

I think about Thanksgiving and Ethan J. Lane. My family is not leaving to Shayla's house until half an hour before we start the feast. So Ethan is going to hide out at my house.

My dad and I are going to pick him up at the small airport nearby. The small airport is in Witchport, California. It is about a twenty five minute drive from here.

We plan on getting home with about fifteen to twenty minutes to spare before heading over to Shayla's house for the feast.

My mind traces back to the thought of planes and airports. I have a seriously bad fear of heights and I am terribly claustrophobic. Put me on a plane and I would nearly have a heart attack. I actually probably would.

I am really excited for Thanksgiving tomorrow. I get to meet more of Shayla's family and my favorite author.

With the luck Shayla, Zachery and I have had, this Thanksgiving is unpredictable. Really, the world may never know what happens.

A Nanowrimo Novel

Invisible Thoughts

Anyway, we should still live it like our last day.
Which for one, is possibly last.

A Nanowrimo Novel

Chapter 19 Ethan

I always get fan-mail but never like the one Walton sent me. Even though Zachery is not his brother, or cousin, or any type of relative, he still took the time to write me a three page e-mail on his adventures with Zachery and Shayla. Even though I am going to Peacock, California to surprise Zachery, I have a surprise in mind for Walton too.

I am very surprised at the thing the three kids have gone through in less than two months. So surprised and impressed to the point I want to write a novel about it. The novel won't be that long of course, it only covers two months. At least for now.

I wait at the airport for Walton and his father to pick me up. I sit on the bench outside the small airport under the shade. Even though winter is around the corner in northern California, it is around sixty degrees in Witchport, California.

I originally come from East Point, Maine. It is a smaller, serene, town in the south east part of Maine.

I used to act out my book when I was younger. Once I got to old to play make believe, I started to write.

I always used to give up on writing my book. I would get about a thousand words in, then just quit. Once I got older, I decided to go all the way through.

Nowadays, I live in Honolulu, Hawaii. I flew in to San Francisco and from there, I flew to Witchport.

A car pulls up to the curb and I rise from my seat to see if it's Walton. I don't know what he looks like but he knows what I look like seeing I am a famous writer. For that inconvenience, we made a special code on how we know it's each other.

A teenage boy hops out of the car. And walks up to me. He stands a couple feet away from me as I wait for him to say something.

"Operation Zachery?" The boy asks

It is Walton. That was our code to distinguish each other.

"Nice to meet you Walton Coy." I go over and shake his hand.

He smiles and greets me back. Walton lets me have the front passenger seat and he takes the back.

"Hello, nice to meet you Mr.Lane." The man who says that is probably Walton's dad.

"Hello sir, nice to meet you to Mr.Coy."

We smile at each other then get on our way. Walton, on the way to Peacock, keeps asking me weird questions that relate to my book and what sounds like real life problems for him. Seeing what ht told for a story, he is trying to clear up questions about that Callum kid and his tall friend who's name is presently unknown.

I know I want to help Walton with his case on the suspected drug dealers but, I just don't know how. Then it hits me.

"Walton?" I question.

"Yeah?"

"I got a question for you this time."

"You know how the main character in my book quickly takes down the villain by being sly and smart?"

"Well, yeah."

"Well Walton, that should answer all the questions over all."

"I get what your saying, keep going."

I turn my head and look straight at Walton as he grins. I speak again.

"Hope you're a good photographer Walton cause thats how we are going to win it."

He just looks at me confused. I have been planing a solution to the problem the whole time while I was in flight. Walton and I sneak over to that hideout, catch them red handed, taking a couple snaps, turn the pics into the police, and were finished, the mayhem stops right there. Right there.

Chapter 20 Walton

I thought about Ethan's answer the rest of the way home as he talked to dad about politics and Hawaii. I never knew Ethan lives in Hawaii.

I get a call from Shayla the next moment. I reach for my phone in my back pocket.

"Hey Walton, Uncle Flynn just got here, Zachery is amazed in happily excited. How is your pick up going?"

"Great! We got the surprise guest in the car and were five minutes away from my house."

"Perfect, head over anytime."

"Okay, sounds good, be there soon, bye Shayla."

"Okay, bye Walton."

I hang up the phone call and just place the phone to my side. I look out the car window. We just entered Peacock, California. It takes us three minutes from entering the town of Peacock to get to our destination.

By the time we get home, Ethan gets his luggage out of the back of the car, and he settles into his temporary room for the next three nights, then it is time to head to Shayla's house.

Once we get to Shayla's house, Zachery is already stoked about his Uncle Flynn. He may have a heart attack once Ethan walks in. Which, nearly happens.

I walk through the door first. Then my father. My mother has already arrived at the Blue's household earlier because she did not come with my dad and I to pick up Ethan.

Once Ethan enters the door, Zachery is screaming, jumping up and down. Ethan strides over to Zachery and shakes his hand when he calms down.

"You must be the extraordinary Zachery that Walton told me about. Am I right?"

Zachery nods his head speedily at Ethan, happy and surprised to see him. Ethan and Zachery start to talk up a storm and head to the living room to do so. I decide I will introduce myself to this Uncle Flynn guy that Shayla was talking about.

I head to the dining room to find Shayla and who must be Uncle Flynn because I have never seen him before.

"Hey Walton, have you met my Uncle Flynn?" Shayla gestures for me to walk over to the other side of the dining room table to sit down with her and her Uncle Flynn.

Shayla sits at the head of the table as her Uncle Flynn sits on her right side. I take a seat on her left side.

"Nice to meet you Walton, I have heard all good about you." Shayla's Uncle sounds very enthusiastic while talking. He sort of reminds me of Mrs.Abagail.

"Nice to meet you too Uncle Flynn."

"Just call me Flynn, I don't mind."

"Ok then, nice to meet you Flynn."

The three of us sit at the dining room table and talk about Zachery's cancer until everyone else starts to pile in.

Shayla, Flynn and I keep the seats we already have as the others find their own seats. My mother sits next to me as Shayla's mother sits next to her.

On the other side of the table, Zachery sits next to Flynn and Ethan sits next to Zachery on his other side. Shayla's father sits next to Ethan as my father sits next to him. We are all seated and ready to feast.

We all start to pass the bowls of food around the table. I eat some turkey with mashed potato and cranberry sauce. Mostly everyone else's plate looks the same as mine but maybe with a little more of something or a little less of something.

Nobody really talks while eating. We just eat. We all eat really slow for the most part, taking in the good meal we all prepared. We do eat slow until my mom asks if anybody is ready for desert.

For desert, we have apple pie. Everybody takes a slice of the pie to eat. We all finish desert in less than twelve minutes at the most.

"Thank you all for this great meal." Flynn speaks as he goes around to pick up everybody's plates.

"Agreed." Admitted Shayla's mother from the kitchen, washing dishes.

Ethan and Zachery head back to the living room to continue their conversation on Ethan's book.

Shayla, Flynn and I stay in the dining room as everyone else cleans up in the kitchen.

"So Flynn, you came to visit from Ohio, am I right?" I question Flynn about where he came from.

"Yep, I did. And you live here in Peacock?"

"Yes I do."

"Do you and Shayla go to the same school?"

"Yes we do. We are also in all the same classes."

"That must be nice to have your best friend in your class all day."

"It sure is."

My family (With the exception of Ethan) head out around seven P.M. I am used to having Thanksgiving dinner in the afternoon so this is different for my family and I.

Once I get home, Ethan already has plans for the rest of the night. He told my parents we were going to walk around town and I would be his tour guide but he told me that we are going to go on a secret mission to end the Callum case once and for all.

I told Ethan we could end the Callum case tomorrow but he insists on ending it tonight. I finally convince him to go tomorrow.

Ethan and I make our way to the kitchen to have a late night snack. I find it odd how we just ate the Thanksgiving feast at Shayla house, and yet, we are already hungry to eat again.

"So Walton." Ethan turns his head to me as we sit at the table in the kitchen. I open my small pack of peanut crackers at the same time he does. We have the same taste in snack.

"Have a good camera ready for tomorrow night. We will need it to end the Callum case once and for all."

"Ethan, how the heck can a camera end the mess between three kids and two drug dealers?"

"Well Walton, put it this way, it captures life's moments."

Chapter 21 Walton

The next night comes by super fast it seems like. It is eleven P.M and my parents are asleep. Ethan and I have our black attire on, ready to stop crime. I find it funny how an author and a teenage boy are about to stop crime.

I have my mothers fancy, sharp, precise camera in my hand and my phone in my back pocket. Ethan told me that once we see those thugs, I snap a couple pictures with both my phone and the camera then we sprint back to his rental car he got this morning.

We make our way downstairs, being so quiet that you could hear dead skin fall off of us. A little over the top with the exaggeration, but whatever.

I slowly and quietly open the front door of the house, wanting to be as quiet as possible. Ethan makes his way out first and I follow and shut the door behind us.

Ethan remotely unlocks his car and takes to the driver's seat. I make my way to the front passenger seat, finally, unlike with Shayla all those times, I finally get to sit in the front.

Ethan's rental car is a two thousand and eight black Dodge Charger. It lights up inside with colorful buttons and switches.

The two of us are quiet while we drive towards the dark ally way. We don't even play the radio on the ride there.

The only sound is the car and the other cars around us. By the time we make it to the ally way, it is eleven fifteen, and we are ready to go.

Ethan and I hop out of the car quietly and quickly, wanting to be very sly. We slowly close our car doors and Ethan remotely locks the car.

We creep towards the hideout of Callum and his friend, weary to be cautious and have are ears perked at all times.

We stop when we are in sight of the door that I ran into last time. Ethan snatches the camera out of my hands as I take my phone out.

As we start to creep towards the door a little more, a hand pulls me from behind, putting me in a choke hold.

I also see Ethan being put in choke hold. Again? This time Shayla is not here to back me up. This could be the end of Walton and Ethan, not the Callum case.

A Nanowrimo Novel

Invisible Thoughts

A Nanowrimo Novel

Chapter 22 Zachery

I let out a blood curdling scream as I quickly jerk up in bed. My whole body aches all over as I keep my scream going.

Uncle Flynn is the first to enter my room. He is followed by Shayla and my parents.

"I am dying!" I scream "I am dying!"

Well what I said gives my mother a heart attack. Literally.

My father goes to my mothers aide.

"Shayla and Flynn! Get Zachery to the hospital! I'll take care of mom! Now! Go!"

Why doesn't mom come with us? Is she really having a heart attack? Maybe it is just my mind going dead with the rest of me. But if dad said he will take care of mom?

I shake the thought out of my head and focus on staying alive.

Shayla is carrying me down the stairs as Uncle Flynn races ahead of us. Uncle Flynn heads outside with no shoes on but manages to snatch moms car keys of the table in the kitchen.

Shayla runs me outside then into moms Camry. I am gently placed in the back. I don't even bother to buckle up. I do not think it is going to make a difference.

Uncle Flynn takes the drivers seat as Shayla sits in the back with me.

I am crying and have my knees brought up to my head. my whole body aches. I do not have my prosthetic leg on. It is back in my room inside the house.

Uncle Flynn is half way to the hospital in a flash. Shayla is whispering to me, saying that everything is going to be all right.

All of the sudden, everything amazing that has ever happened to me rushes through my head. Living back in Ohio, living here in Peacock, California. Also all the people that mean something to me to. Shayla, mom, dad, Uncle Flynn. Walton and Ethan even cross about my mind. I wonder what their doing?

My eyes and mind start to drift off, wander away. I feel like I am dying. If this is what it feels like.

"Shayla, am I dying?" It takes all the strength I have left in me to say those words.

Invisible Thoughts

Shayla looks at me with a small smile. I know she is not happy that I am dying, but happy I will be going off to another place.
"Well Zachery, that's up to you."

A Nanowrimo Novel

Chapter 23 Walton

I am not falling to Callum and his friends strength again. Not again. I quickly elbow the man that has a hold of me in what I think is the face. He groans in pain.

Ethan does the same thing and elbows his man holding him. Ethan and I stand together looking at our work.

The two males look like they are having seizures on the ground.

I walk up to the one I think is Callum and kick him square in the face. He starts to whimper and hold his face. I feel guilt when he holds his face.

"Well played, Eric." Says the man who I just kicked. "You say we could catch them but they caught us."

The one that was holding Ethan just looks at the one I kicked. He must be Eric. He must be Callum's friend.

"Sorry Callum. You have made mistakes too you know." Eric spits at Callum and hits him in the arm.

I hand Ethan my phone and he dials 9-1-1. Now I know the Callum case is over. Ethan and I run back to his car and at the same time, Ethan is on my phone making a report to the cops. *We did it.* I think to myself. *We did it, it's over.*

Epilogue
2 Years Later

As Shayla and I drive to the graveyard, I think about the past couple years. I think about meeting Shayla, meeting Zachery and Callum. And, I think about that one night when everything broke loose.

On that night exactly 2 years ago, Ethan Lane and I stopped Callum and Eric while Shayla and her Uncle Flynn were trying to rush Zachery to the hospital but he died on the way. Why they didn't call the ambulance? I don't know. Why didn't Ethan and I call the cops before hand? I don't know. That night, everything went haywire.

In the past two years since then, Shayla and I got our licenses, Ethan released a new novel, Shayla's dad got a job as a teacher at the elementary school, and my mother got a promotion at her bank.

We buried Zachery in one of the next towns over called Spruce Wood. It is a much nicer town then Peacock and it is more of a serene place to bury some one. Spruce Wood is a very small town and has this one small, beautiful graveyard, the graveyard in which Zachery is buried.

Shayla turns off the radio as we pull into the graveyard. Zachery is in the way back, still the newest edition to the place.

I am the first to get out of the car when it stops. Zachery's grave sits in the back, as peaceful as ever.

Fake Flowers and pictures of Zachery sit all around the gravestone, making it look nice.

Shayla hops out of the car now, she walks around the car with a set of real flowers. She gently place the flowers in front of the name Zachery Blue engraved on the front of the gravestone.

I see Shayla wipe away some tears so I go and stand next to her.

"It was all my fault, I should have called the ambulance and Zachery could still be here." Shayla cries a little as she turns to talk to me.

"Shayla it is not your fault, everything happens with a reason."

"Then what reasoning does this have Walton?" Shayla looks me straight in the eyes with disgust.

"The reasoning for this has probably not been solved. Some things are never solved Shayla and you know that."

"When we finally got him to the hospital, they couldn't figure out exactly what killed him but they swear it had to do with his cancer."

"Shayla, I am so sorry. You do not need to talk about this if you do not want to, seriously."

"No, I want to talk about this, I do. I was sitting in the back of the car with him. He was groaning in pain. I din't know what to do, if there was something I could have done to save him I would have done it in a heartbeat but there was nothing to my knowledge."

"Shayla, seriously, you don't need to talk about this."

Shayla keeps going though, even though I told her she doesn't have to.

"It seems like your night two years ago went better. You got the thugs in jail and then, found their old boss who still sold drugs after Callum took over with his friend. Is his name Eric?"

"Yep. His name is Eric."

"You and Ethan had it made Walton while Uncle Flynn and I did not."

The two of us become pretty quiet for a minute or two after Shayla finishes her spiel about today two years ago.

The past two years have seemed normal. Shayla fits right into Californian life now, we have both graduated high school and are both starting college next year, separating from each other and our families, but it just all seems normal to me.

I am going to college in Witchport, were we picked up Ethan. The college there is smaller then most and specializes in mechanics. I am going there to get a degree in mechanics and then open my own repair shop.

Shayla is going off to Harvard in Massachusetts. It is certainly a long way off but the college is paying for most of it because they want her there for her intelligence. She is going for history. She wants to be a history professor at Harvard University. She told me that has been her life long dream.

"Walton, lets get going, everybody is waiting for us back at my house."

"Okay, but you are driving."

Since Zachery has died, for the past two years, for Thanksgiving and Christmas Flynn and Ethan come by to celebrate with us. Ethan is like family now to me. He stays at my house like the first time and makes himself right at home.

Flynn is like the step brother I never had. He turns out to be really funny and is never serious. This Thanksgiving, he "accidentally" shook the salt shaker all over me. He claims he mistook me for his plate. Is he blind? I now have two things set in the back of my mind about him. The first, not to sit next to him next year at Thanksgiving and the second one, I need to get revenge before he leaves.

As Shayla and I drive down the road I think about Zachery and how much fun he use to be. I think about the obstacle race, being stuck in the dumpster with him, being caught with him, how smart he was, he was overall the most amazing person I have ever met.

I wonder if Shayla just stops her whole world around her and thinks about Zachery. She must. It is her brother after all. She surely talks about him a lot. When we are driving in the car, sitting in the living room, anytime, anywhere. One time at the Thanksgiving fair, we were in the ferris wheel and she started talking about Zachery. She is just random.

Once we make it back to Shayla's house, it is two in the afternoon. Both Ethan and Flynn's rental cars sit in the driveway along with Shayla's dads vehicle. Shayla and I have her mothers car.

I walk in behind Shayla, careful that Flynn may be pulling some prank on me. As I walk in, I look to my left, I figure out I looked the wrong way when Flynn comes at me from my right and tackles me to the ground. This is his form of greeting me.

"Hey Walton, how did you like today's greeting?" Flynn laughs at me hysterically as he pins me to the floor.

"You idiot! Get off me!" I kick Flynn just barely and push him as I get up. Flynn decides to stay on the ground and sits cross legged. He looks like such a doofus as he sits by the door.

I make my way to the kitchen were the only soul is Ethan. Both Ethan and Flynn are heading back to their own homes tomorrow morning.

"How are you doing Walton?" Ethan has his arm supported against the island as he sits at a chair.

"The usual with a bit of grief and sorrow."

"Well, how did Shayla do, she hasn't been there since last year?"

"She got a little mad and sad at once but she tok it well."

Ethan stands up and walks over to me.

"Walton, lets take a walk."

Ethan and I make our way outside, walking to who knows where.

Ethan ends up leading me to the inner city part of Peacock. We end up at the fountain in the middle of the buildings and people. We sit at the bench closest to the fountain.

"Walton, I still can't get over that story of you, Shayla and Zachery." Ethan looks at me enthusiastically. I roll my eyes at him.

"Hey, you know it was amazing Walton." Ethan answers back to my rolling of the eyes.

"Alright Ethan, I will give in just this once."

"Why thank you for letting me have this victory Walton Coy."

"No problem Ethan Lane."

We laugh a little then look towards the fountain. The fountain is pretty big. It sort of has two layers to it. Two layers that I can't really explain. Water trickles down the whole thing, finding a new home in the pool of water beneath it.

A small little girl walks up to the fountain with what looks like a penny in her hands. Then it hits me. It is Sarah Leopold.

I haven't seen Sarah Leopold for two years. Her hair is a little curly and comes down a little past her shoulders. She wears a long, pink winter coat with furry boots. She seems to be happy by the looks of it.

Sarah looks pretty happy as she flips the penny into the fountain. That makes me think about just hopelessly falling into water.

The penny makes a small splash as it hits the waters surface.

"Is that the little girl that is the sister of one of the bullies?" Ethan talks very lightly under his breath.

"Sarah Leopold. Little sister of Lucien Leopold." I whisper back to Ethan.

Sarah seems to spot me out in the crowd. *Great.* She starts to skip over to Ethan and I. This is just what we need. The little girl that is kind of the only problem left of the Callum case talking to us. But to my surprise, she goes right pass Ethan and I. Not even looking at us. That works out.

"Walton, I have a life long task I made for you." Ethan starts to whisper again as we rise from our seats on the benches.

"Well, what is it that you ask of me?"

Ethan and I start to make our way back to Shayla's house as we talk. Then, Ethan stops abruptly in the middle of everything it feels like. He stopped in the middle of my life, his life, and everyone else's.

"Walton, I want you to live your life in description and to the fullest. No matter what happens to you, you keep on trucking. Follow your dreams and never give up. That is obviously what you are here for, this is your destiny."

"What is my destiny?"

"To be who you want to be and get the best out of it."

The rest of the walk back to Shayla's house is pretty quiet. I am thinking about what Ethan said and I want to do all those things for him and everyone else in my life. How will I? I do not know quite yet. Who will rally with me? I guess I'll have to find out.

I was right from the beginning, life can be challenging. I took down drug dealers, helped a kid with cancer live life to the fullest, and most importantly made new friends. All of those events in my life happened in less then two months and I wish I could go back to those two months. They were the best two months of my life. It is two years later now and I need to move on from those two months and live the life that is right in front of me. That is what Ethan J. Lane, my favorite author wants from me, right?

The End

Invisible Thoughts

A Nanowrimo Novel

Made in the USA
Lexington, KY
27 February 2015